A.L.F. Resort
Artificial Life Form

Holly Copella

In loving memory of
Nana & PapPap Werner

ACKNOWLEDGMENTS

Copella Books: First Paperback Edition 2018
Printed by CreateSpace, An Amazon.com Company
Cover Artist: Daniela Owergoor
Dani-owergoor.deviantart.com

PUBLISHER'S NOTE

Chapter One

The two-hundred foot, twin-screw diesel yacht was anchored half a mile from the secluded beach dock. The four-deck yacht contained six bedroom suites, a pool, and a hot tub. The expensive ship had few lights lit both inside and out. The dark ocean was still, and the nighttime sky was clear with a nearly full moon and brilliant stars. A woman's panic-stricken scream broke the silence. A young, terrified woman ran along the ship's deck. The once attractive woman now appeared haggard from her recent ordeal.

"Detective!" Kim screamed while running. "He's here!"

The woman in her mid-thirties attempted to run in her sundress and bare feet. She'd already lost her shoes while attempting to maintain her balance. A large, intimidating man ran after her with a Bowie knife clutched in his hand. The killer was over six foot four and built like a lineman. If he caught her, he was going to do a lot more than tackle her. His shaved head and the large scar on the left side of his face gave him a menacing look as if the look in his eyes wasn't menacing enough. He was repulsive to the point of being hideous. Kim looked back, saw the violent man with the knife closing in on her then screamed and darted into the nearby lounge through the port side door.

The breathtaking lounge had windows on both sides for a panoramic view of the ocean, several oversized chairs, and a small wet bar. Despite its grandeur, Kim wasn't able to enjoy the luxury. She slammed the door behind her and immediately backed away from it. The killer slammed against the door, vibrating it to the point of nearly breaking it. The sound immediately stopped after one hit. Kim held her breath while staring at the door, hoping he'd given up his pursuit. She nervously reached for the doorknob then immediately pulled her hand back. It was a trick! She turned and ran across the lounge for the second door on the aft side.

"Detective," she again screamed.

She threw open the aft side door and jumped back with alarm as the killer slashed his knife at her. Kim again screamed and slammed the door shut. She ran in the opposite direction and through another set of doors, entering an interior corridor. She heard a loud thumping just down the hall.

"Kim," a man cried out from behind the door. "Kim!"

"Detective," she cried with relief and practically slid into the door.

Kim attempted to open the door, but it wouldn't budge. The killer appeared in the corridor and ran toward her with a crazed look in his eyes. Kim screamed and slammed her shoulder into the door before her, attempting to free the detective. When the door didn't budge, she grabbed a nearby fire extinguisher then hesitated. She saw the ax in the glass case alongside it. Kim tossed the fire extinguisher aside and broke the glass. She grabbed the ax and struck the door near the doorknob, splintering the door. The killer was nearly upon her. Kim screamed and turned to face him with the ax in her hands.

"You want me?" she cried out as her rage surfaced. "Come on!"

The killer slashed at her with the Bowie knife. Kim screamed and frantically waved the ax rather than swing it. The killer placed his foot on her abdomen and thrust her backward to the floor. The ax flew from her hands and slid across the corridor. The large man moved over her and was about to stab her. Kim screamed hysterically. A door was heard cracking. The killer looked back. A man in a trench coat plowed into the killer and took him to the floor. Detective Austin was a fairly handsome man in his late thirties with dark, thinning hair and two days of facial stubble. He scrambled to his feet and pulled Kim back just in time to avoid the killer's knife as it struck the floor. They bolted down the hallway as the killer jumped to his feet.

Detective Austin saw the discarded ax on the floor and grabbed it. The killer lunged for them while swinging his knife at Austin. Detective Austin gasped with alarm and swung the ax while shutting his eyes. The ax struck the killer in the chest, splitting through bone and narrowly missing his heart. The killer stumbled backward despite the blood seeping past the ax and attempted to slash Detective Austin with the knife. Detective Austin pulled Kim into his arms while both stared in horror as the killer stumbled backward with the ax still in his chest. It seemed impossible that he was still alive. He finally fell to the floor and no longer moved. Both exhaled with relief.

"I don't know about you, Detective Austin," she announced while gasping, "but I'm glad this vacation is over."

"Yeah, me too."

They looked at each other and managed a soft chuckle. Detective Austin smiled gently then kissed her warmly. The sound of sirens could be heard in the distance.

Chapter Two

The police boat carrying Detective Austin and Kim returned to the dock as a second patrol boat docked with the impressive yacht. Several men climbed onboard and fanned out along the deck. Their black jackets had the bold writing 'SWAT' on the back. Within the yacht's corridor, a man in a white lab coat kneeled over the dead killer. Ross Stockton was an average looking man in his early forties with some graying along the temples of his dark hair. He removed the bloodied ax from the dead man and handed it to his assistant, who placed it in a large bag.

"I hate ax wounds," Ross informed his assistant. "If that damned detective hadn't lost his electronic pulse gun, it would have saved me a lot of work."

Ross removed the base of the killer's skull to reveal the complex computer system within the killer's head. Every gizmo and gadget remained dark. Ross plugged an electronic device into the motherboard. Every light within the computer system turned on, and the killer's eyes opened. Ross returned the cover to the base of the killer's skull and casually stood. The killer stood as well.

"Okay, back to the lab for repairs, big guy," Ross announced while sighing.

The killer walked with some difficulty along the corridor and accidentally walked into the wall.

Ross' eyes widened in horror. "Oh, no," he cried out. "Don't you dare malfunction. I'm not carrying your heavy ass all the way back to the lab. Move it out."

The killer continued to stagger along the corridor while Ross followed. A cleaning crew immediately sprang into action and cleaned the fake blood left behind.

§

The following morning, Detective Austin and Kim arrived at the dock with their arms around each other in a loving embrace. They approached the awaiting watercraft. The dock was only one of two ways on and off the island for vacationing guests. Although some guests arrived by boat, most chose the faster route via the watercraft. Despite only accommodating six passengers, the guests enjoyed the luxury of the smaller craft allowing for a scenic trip from the mainland. A neatly dressed man in his forties waited before the watercraft and greeted the happy couple. Delaney Todd, the resort owner, was a tall, lean man with slightly gray, thinning hair. His wealth and expensive taste in clothes made him seem more handsome than he actually was. He grinned and greeted the couple.

"How did you enjoy your fantasy vacation at A.L.F. Resort?" Delaney asked cheerfully.

"Exhausting." Kim informed him while laughing. "But it was the best vacation of my life."

Detective Austin placed his arm around Kim, affectionately clung to her, and smiled. "I don't think it's over just yet."

Delaney chuckled warmly in response. "We love to hear about our guests developing relationships off the island," he announced, pleased with their budding romance.

Not all the resorts hook-ups worked out according to the fantasy planner's design, but they certainly had their share of blooming romances, which made guests happy. Happy guests gave raving reviews; and raving reviews brought more guests.

"I can't thank you enough," Austin replied cheerfully then nuzzled Kim, who immediately giggled.

They again shook hands with Delaney then boarded the watercraft. Delaney smiled his approval then turned and headed back along the dock toward his awaiting, luxury golf cart. He passed a large sign at the end of the dock that read, "A.L.F. Resort. Artificial Life Form."

Chapter Three

The airport was moderately congested despite the early morning hour. An attractive woman in her mid-twenties sat near the large windows overlooking the tarmac as she typed on her laptop. Shay Temple was the newly appointed feature writer for Quest Magazine. Shay was the typical girl-next-door with her long auburn hair tied back in a ponytail and just a touch of make-up. Her travel companion and co-worker, Becka Darcy, approached while fiddling with her large digital camera. Becka was a raven-haired beauty in her late twenties. Her dark eyes and eyelashes allowed her to go makeup free and still attract plenty of male attention.

"I love airports," Becka announced cheerfully, despite the early hour.

Shay glanced up at her friend. "Which part? The crowds or the germs?"

"You know, you're on vacation," Becka remarked and collapsed into the chair alongside her co-worker. "You're supposed to be having fun."

"We're on assignment, not a vacation," Shay reminded her.

Becka groaned. "Okay, a work-cation."

Shay resumed her work on the laptop and studied it with fascination. "According to my research on A.L.F. Resort, there are usually two hundred or less human guests in any given week, and out of that, only about ten to twenty request the fantasy package. They only have approximately one hundred human employees." She glanced up and eyed her friend. "The rest are all A.L.F.s."

"A.L.F.s," Becka scoffed and rolled her eyes. "What a name. Makes me think of furry creatures from outer space." She sat forward and grinned with giddy delight. "So--when are you going to tell me?"

"Tell you what?"

"What you put in the questionnaire," Becka pried.

Shay shrugged. "Nothing specific."

Becka groaned and collapsed into her seat. "God, you are so boring."

She sharply eyed her friend. "Anything has to be better than what you requested."

"The magazine is giving us an all-expense paid vacation to check out this resort, and you're being a party-pooper," Becka insisted.

"It's *not* a vacation."

"I'm not allowed to take any pictures," Becka informed her. "It's a vacation."

Shay found something interesting on her laptop. "It says here they're coming out with a new A.L.F. model," she announced with enthusiasm. "The Gen X. The Gen X is so realistic; it's nearly impossible to tell it from a human and has fewer glitches."

There was an awkward silence as Becka stared at Shay, who remained engrossed in her research. "Is it true about their, uh, sexual capabilities?"

Shay suddenly eyed her friend as her mouth hung open. "Please don't tell me you're going to get it on with an A.L.F.," she practically gasped. "With the nature of your twisted fantasy, that would make me sick."

"I didn't say that," Becka remarked with a huff. "I was just curious if it's true. Can you have sex with the A.L.F.s?"

"Yes, they're designed for intercourse," Shay replied then muttered, "Some perverted man's idea, I'm sure. Ten million dollar dildos."

Becka giggled. "Okay, now you're just turning me on."

Shay suddenly eyed her friend. "Oh, my God," she gasped. "You are thinking about it!"

"Come on, you can't tell me you're not curious," Becka announced while grinning.

"No, I'm not thinking about it," Shay insisted. "Although after Jason, I'm sure a robot would be an improvement."

"It's been a year. Forget about your loser college ex," Becka announced. "He was a jerk and didn't deserve you. I think you should find yourself a real man. A ten million dollar A.L.F. man." She then considered her comment. "If A.L.F.s are completely realistic, I wonder if they only last two minutes then roll over and fall asleep?"

"Okay, not another word about sex with A.L.F.s," Shay scoffed then made a face. "You're creeping me out. Considering your fantasy request, I'd think sex would be the last thing on that warped mind of yours."

"At least I'm going to give you something worth writing about when we get back," Becka remarked. "Your fantasy is going to put your readers to sleep."

Shay groaned softly and finally gave in. "I requested a spy adventure."

Becka turned in her seat and rested her temple on her fist with giddy delight. "Really? Hmm, that sounds spicy."

"Don't get your hopes up," Shay scolded. "I specifically requested no romance. I know how this resort works. They're known for playing matchmaker with the guests. The last thing I need is a man in my life."

Becka chuckled while grinning. "Huh, that's what you need most."

Shay glared at Becka while she laughed.

Chapter Four

The elegant resort property was nestled along the white, sandy beach and offered a romantic, sunny backdrop no matter what fantasy the guest requested. The hotel itself wasn't nearly as large as other hotels on beachfront property, but it also didn't accommodate many guests on a weekly basis. Due to the nature of its clientele, the resort catered to only a dozen or more fantasy guests, although guests could stay at the resort on a non-fantasy vacation and still have interaction with the A.L.F.s. As with any expensive resort, it offered nearly every amenity conceivable from indoor and outdoor swimming pools, isolated hot tubs with romantic views, tennis courts, gardens, clubs, restaurants, and a large spa.

Beyond the resort, there was an entire city void of life, giving the rest of the island an almost creepy appeal. The city was broken up into staging areas. Each staging area allowed guests to continue with their fantasy vacation free from interruptions. Within the resort itself, there was a spacious lobby, dance clubs, restaurants, banquet halls, and luxury suites. An entire wing was devoted to security and the daily operations of a highly computerized resort.

Delaney sat behind his large, mahogany desk within his corner office and studied his laptop with his usual seriousness. Ross and another man in a lab coat sat before the desk. George Lambert was Ross' second in command in the science division in charge of keeping the A.L.F.s operational.

"Our guests from Quest Magazine will be here this afternoon," he informed them. "I can't stress how important it is for our guest reporter and her photographer to have the most fantastic time of their lives this week." He then eyed Ross and George. "Is everything set up for Becka Darcy's fantasy?"

"We pulled out all the stops on this one," Ross informed him. "Although I'll be surprised if she has enough nerve to finish the entire week."

"Sounds promising. What about Shay Temple?" Delaney asked and leaned forward on his desk. "She's a real skeptic. Do we have an amazing time planned for her?"

"To the last detail," George announced proudly. "Our spy is going to rock her world."

"Remember, it can't look like a romantic set-up," Delaney insisted. "She specifically asked for no romance. How are we on subtle?"

"We're very subtle with this one," George responded. "Trust me; it's a match made in heaven."

"She's going to meet our new model Gen X as well," Ross announced proudly. "He's going to blow her mind."

Delaney groaned and shook his head, showing less enthusiasm. "You and your Gen X," he muttered. "I hope it's worth all the money you've put into it." He then sat back in his chair and eyed Ross with disapproval. "Why do you insist on referring to your A.L.F.s as he and she?"

"Since they have vaginas or testicles, I think it's only fair to call them he and she," Ross insisted, although he was obviously offended when his creations were criticized. "We've put a lot of money into making them fully functioning he and she's. I would think you'd appreciate the effort, considering you're the highest paid pimp in the world."

"I hate when you talk like that," Delaney muttered.

Ross smiled and shrugged.

"Ross' Gen X is so lifelike; it's almost impossible to tell he isn't human," George boasted. "His responses are amazingly real, and we haven't found a single glitch in his actions or speech."

"Yeah, so why didn't you make him look like Brad Pitt?" Delaney demanded.

"That's the beauty of the Gen X," Ross insisted, seemingly proud of the fact. "If he's too perfect, he's not as believable. We went for average on purpose."

"Well, if it works as you think it should, I want them drop-dead gorgeous," Delaney insisted. "Our guests are paying for it, and they want handsome men and gorgeous women." He suddenly hesitated and considered his comment. "God, I am a pimp."

Chapter Five

Ross and George walked along the corridor toward their office with their morning coffee while joking around about their earlier meeting with the boss. An attractive, well-dressed woman in her late twenties with long, golden blonde hair seemed engrossed in the state-of-the-art, 5"x7" tablet she held. She walked a few lengths ahead of them and turned the corner into another corridor. Penny was essentially Delaney's right-hand person and kept the resort running smoothly as far as the guests were concerned. George stared at the attractive woman and appeared anxious.

"I'll catch up with you later," he announced.

"George, don't," Ross groaned while frowning. "She dumped you. Let it go."

"I'm just going to talk to her." George hurried to catch up to Penny and walked alongside her. He managed a pleasant smile. "Hey, Penny."

Penny didn't bother looking up from her tablet, but her expression relayed her intentions. "I'm busy, George."

"I just want to talk," George insisted. "Can't we even talk anymore?"

Penny looked up and met his gaze, showing little emotion. "The women from Quest Magazine are going to be here in an hour," she bluntly informed him. "I need to make sure everything is perfect for their arrival."

"I just want to know if there's someone else," George blurted out. "I think I have a right to know if you're dumping me for another guy."

Penny groaned and rolled her eyes with annoyance. "We're not having this discussion," she scoffed. "I don't have time." She picked up her pace and walked away.

George watched her disappear around another corner and frowned. He then hurried back the way he'd come and headed into the lab. The lab was George and Ross' home base. Apart from multiple computer systems, there were several exam tables containing A.L.F.s in need of computer repair. The tables electronically transitioned from horizontal to vertical depending upon their individual needs. There were also exam chairs for lesser repairs. George passed Ross, who worked on the computerized brain of an A.L.F. seated within a chair, and flopped down before the large wall of monitors. George pressed several buttons on the massive security monitor. Ross eyed him suspiciously, uncertainly approached, and watched. Penny appeared on one of the screens.

"That's a no-no," Ross scolded. "We're not supposed to spy on our co-workers, especially the ones we used to date. It's called stalking."

"I don't care," George snarled. "I want to know if she's seeing someone else."

Through the monitor, they watched Penny enter the breakroom. As she approached the coffeemaker, Delaney entered and poured coffee for himself as well.

"Are we ready for our VIP guests?" Delaney asked.

"As ready as we'll ever be," Penny replied then turned to Delaney and offered a reassuring smile.

Delaney groaned softly, pulled her into his arms, and kissed her passionately. Penny returned the kiss while running her hands over his body. Within the lab, Ross and George stared at the screen. They watched with surprise and horror as Penny and Delaney kissed passionately.

"Oh, man. That's cold," Ross muttered. "She's making time with the boss."

"How am I supposed to deal with that?" George suddenly demanded. "I certainly can't punch my boss."

"You can, but you'd better look for another job," Ross remarked. "You wanted to know. Now you know. Let it go. She's not worth it."

George flicked the screen off and frowned.

Chapter Six

Delaney and Penny waited by the dock as the watercraft slowed while approaching. Several bellhops stood by with luxury golf carts waiting to whisk away their new guests. Penny consulted her tablet while maintaining a serious expression.

"If I'm correct--" she began.

A plain looking woman in her mid-forties got out of the plane with the assistance of a bellhop, who immediately took her bags. Jillian was about as plain as a woman could be. Her light brown, shoulder length hair was pulled back into a librarian bun, and she wore glasses on her makeup-free face.

"That would be Jillian Webber," Penny announced while studying the meek woman then consulted her tablet.

"She's going to have a wonderful stay. It's going to be the perfect fantasy."

"A little mild for my taste," Delaney remarked.

A serious looking businessman in an expensive suit got out of the watercraft next. Alden was a tall, moderately well-built man in his late forties with thinning silver hair.

"And that, of course, is Alden Mansfield," Penny announced proudly. "A prosecuting attorney with an amazing track record." She studied her tablet and appeared slightly flustered. "Am I reading this right?"

Delaney suddenly chuckled without looking at her tablet. "Oh, definitely."

Penny's eyes widened in surprise. "Wow, you'd never see that one coming."

An attractive woman in her mid-twenties got out of the plane last. She was a stunning woman with long, strawberry blonde hair and a captivating figure. She wore a revealing dress with dangerously high heels.

"And that's Ella Fremont, our dancing queen," Penny informed Delaney.

"Let's get them some drinks and get them settled in before the rest of our guests arrive," Delaney announced. "I want everything to be perfect for the next arrival."

"Just four more, right?"

"The last four, yes," Delaney replied.

"Only seven fantasy vacations this week?"

"We need a good review to get our summer numbers up for next year," Delaney informed her. "Quest Magazine can either make us or break us. We'll need to devote extra time to our VIP guests if we want that spectacular review. Shay Temple is a skeptic. We need to rock her world."

"Her spy fantasy should do that," Penny informed him. "Our spy is pretty spectacular. Charm, good looks, intelligent, and a successful businessman as well. The whole spy fantasy is his dream too. His travel companion was very helpful in putting it all together. He's perfect for Shay."

"Gotta love the cooperative friend," Delaney remarked.

§

The three newly arriving guests rode in the luxury golf cart with the bellhop while their bags were transported in a utility cart. Jillian was enthusiastic and beamed while Ella and Alden appeared more serious. Jillian could no longer contain her enthusiasm despite her quiet travel companions and turned to face Ella seated alongside her.

"So what's your fantasy week?" Jillian asked Ella.

Ella finally smiled and seemed interested in talking once provoked. "I've always wanted to be a professional dancer," her seriousness returned as she considered the comment. "I hope it's worth the price of admission."

"Maybe if you're not busy, you can attend my wedding," Jillian chirped.

"You're getting married?" Ella gasped with surprise then beamed with enthusiasm for the woman. "Congratulations. I didn't know they catered weddings here."

"Actually it's my dream wedding," Jillian attempted to explain. "I figured it would never happen, so I'm having the wedding I've always wanted."

"That's really a unique fantasy," Ella remarked, although it took a while for her to embrace the fantasy wedding idea fully. "Who's the lucky groom?"

"I haven't met him yet, but he's a prince," Jillian announced and handed Ella a wedding invitation.

She accepted the invitation and glanced at it. "Well, I'll certainly try to make that."

Jillian then glanced at the sole man in their group. "What's your fantasy vacation?"

He didn't even look at Jillian. "It's personal," he scoffed.

Jillian and Ella exchanged looks while raising their brows.

Ella smirked and laughed. "He's getting laid."

As both women giggled at the comment, Alden sneered and attempted to ignore them.

Chapter Seven

The elegant resort lounge was a massive, lavishly decorated room that contained a buffet table with snacks as well as a small bar. Shay and Becka held colorful, fruity drinks while picking at some snacks provided for their private orientation since they appeared to be the only guests within the lounge. Penny entered the lounge and joined them. She offered a pleasant greeting then consulted her tablet.

"Since your fantasy vacations are completely separate concepts, you won't reunite until the end of the week," Penny informed them. "Although, I'm sure you were aware of that."

"Believe me," Shay scoffed then held back her laugh. "I don't want to be anywhere near Becka's fantasy."

"And rightly, you shouldn't," Penny announced then turned to face Becka. "Due to the nature of your fantasy, if at any time you change your mind or it becomes too intense, our staff will be monitoring your progress, and you can announce you'd like a time-out or even terminate the fantasy. Use the phrase 'end program' or 'terminate program', and we'll immediately shut down the fantasy. You should be aware that there are cameras everywhere to ensure your safety at all times."

"Are there cameras in all areas?" Shay asked then indicated her friend. "Or just for demented people like Becka?"

Penny offered a pleasant smile. "We don't consider anyone's fantasies demented around here. We don't judge," she announced cheerfully. "But, yes, there are cameras in all the areas to ensure our guests are safe. Obviously, there aren't any in the bathrooms or bedrooms, although in some fantasy cases, we do closely monitor the situation even in the bedrooms."

Both women appeared surprised by the admission.

"Can you give a for instance?" Shay asked.

"Some of our guests like things a little, well, rough in nature," Penny explained.

Shay and Becka stared at her and appeared to get her meaning at the same time.

Becka grinned slyly and chuckled. "Oh, that's kinky."

"Again, we don't judge," Penny replied while smiling, "but in those cases, we need to monitor the situation to keep things from getting out of control."

"But your A.L.F.s are incapable of harming humans," Becka stated, although it was more of a question.

"That's correct, but when you're programming an A.L.F. to be aggressive, there are lines you want to make certain aren't crossed," Penny replied. "Take your fantasy, for example. The intensity is going to be high. You may find it exciting, but someone else may find it overwhelming."

"Will I be interacting with any humans during my fantasy vacation?" Becka asked.

"No, you'll be surrounded by A.L.F.s from the moment you enter your staging area," Penny informed her. "You'll be completely confined."

"How big is the area?"

"Four city blocks," Penny replied.

"Wow, that's big," Becka remarked with surprise.

"But Shay will be interacting with A.L.F.s, staff, and other guests at any given time." Penny then turned to Shay. "As your fantasy progresses, you'll be guided into a specially adapted staging area to keep other guests from stumbling into your fantasy. We don't need a guest playing Sherlock Holmes accidentally shooting the A.L.F. in your spy fantasy."

"That makes sense," Shay replied then gave her a curious look. "Do you actually give guests loaded guns? Sounds risky."

"They're not real guns," Penny explained. "They're electronic pulse guns. They look and sound real, but they can only be used on A.L.F.s. The guns fire an electronic pulse that reacts when it strikes any part of the A.L.F.s body. The result is a crude gunshot wound. Our A.L.F.s are programmed with specific trigger points. So if you shoot them in the head or chest, they're programmed to shut down in a way that simulates death."

"I guess you really did think of everything," Becka remarked.

"Sometimes it's a learning curve based on the type of fantasy," Penny replied. "Your fantasy required a lot of tweaking to get the results we wanted."

"Yeah, leave it to Becka to cause headaches," Shay teased then grinned with enthusiasm. "So after we finish our fantasy vacation, we'll be given a tour behind the scenes?"

"Yes, by Delaney himself," Penny replied cheerfully.

Delaney approached with Ross and George and paused before the three women.

"As I promised, ladies, here are my lead programmers," Delaney informed them. "The masterminds behind the A.L.F.s. Ross and George, meet Shay and Becka from Quest Magazine."

They exchanged pleasantries.

George smiled and extended his arm to Becka. "If you're ready, I'll drive you to your staging area."

Becka grinned with giddiness, waved at Shay, and linked onto George's arm.

"Good luck," Shay called after her then muttered loud enough for her to hear, "you crazy bitch."

Becka called back, "I heard that!"

Delaney focused his attention on Shay. "Ross will escort you to your hotel room so you can freshen up before your full evening ahead."

Shay joined Ross and walked with him toward the lounge doors. "So how does this work exactly?"

"You'll be given a few clues after you've had a chance to freshen up in your room," Ross informed her. "Those clues will start the chain of events to your fantasy."

"What if a guest misinterprets the clues?"

"Either an A.L.F. or one of our actors will guide you in the right direction, sort of like when you miss a turn with GPS," Ross teased. "I'm sure Penny told you, we monitor your progress very closely."

"Yes, and I will be checking the bedroom and bathroom for cameras," Shay announced.

Ross chuckled. "I promise you won't find any."

Chapter Eight

There was a knock on Shay's suite door. Her large, elegant room had all the makings of a luxury suite at the finest hotel. It contained a king-sized bed, a wet bar, and a small sitting area with a large, flat screen television. She hurried from the bathroom and across her suite wearing a plush bathrobe while drying her hair. She was about to open the door when she remembered her spy fantasy had already begun. It was time to be suspicious of everyone and everything. She looked through the peek hole, relaxed, and unlocked the door. An enthusiastic bellhop handed her a large box.

"This just arrived for you, Miss Temple."

Shay accepted the package, tipped the young man, and closed the door behind him. She set the box on the nearby chair and removed the attached card.

"Please wear this tonight. H.B."

There was a matchbook for 'Club A.L.F.', which was just a short walk from the main resort. Shay's curiosity was piqued. She opened the box to reveal a sexy, black dress with matching shoes. She suddenly frowned and shook her head.

"Don't you dare turn this into a romantic, spy thriller, boys," she muttered, already seeing it coming.

§

The large, modern building with 'Club A.L.F.' boldly splattered across the marquee seemed to be alive with activity that evening. It was the happening place to be seen while on the island. Fashionably dressed men and women lined up outside to gain access to the popular club. Despite being two stories of dance club, the place was often filled to the maximum capacity with both humans and A.L.F.s. Considering the resort was all-inclusive, the free drinks didn't dissuade the crowds any. The throngs of guests danced, drank, and had a good time to the loud, club music. The resort also offered several lounges in the main building for the older crowd, who didn't require blaring music for a good time.

Two fashionably dressed men, Hunt Bennett and Murphy Simon, stood by the bar and studied the club scene. Hunt was a handsome, athletically built man in his late twenties with light brown hair that nearly touched his collar. Murphy was a ruggedly handsome man, also in his late twenties, but built slightly more muscular than his friend. His brown hair was neatly trimmed, although his face contained more than a days' worth of stubble. The dance floor was packed with young people strutting their stuff. The main attraction, though, was a fiery new dancer, Ella. She wore a skimpy, eye-catching dress that revealed plenty of leg and more than enough cleavage while she danced on one of the small stages. She danced seductively to the music and gained much-desired attention. As promised, she was a dancing star.

Murphy and Hunt watched the attractive woman dancing on stage a moment longer then focused their attention on the crowded club.

"How many A.L.F.s are there in here?" Murphy asked while looking around.

"Can't be many, but I'd swear there were a limited number of actual humans at the resort," Hunt remarked then appeared curious as he looked around the crowded dance floor. "That's a lot of A.L.F.s. How do you tell them from the live people?"

"According to our welcome pack, which you obviously didn't read," Murphy teased, "A.L.F.s have green eyes, and they wear their signature watches or bracelets with the official A.L.F. logo on them."

"I did read the welcome packet, I just stopped at 'sexually functional'," Hunt announced while chuckling with humor. "I couldn't get that out of my mind in order to finish reading the welcome packet."

Murphy glared at his friend and shook his head. "You paid a lot of money for a spy fantasy, remember?" he demanded. "Are you still on that whole sexually functional kick?"

"That I can have sex with a robot? Yes, I'm still on that," Hunt boldly remarked and grinned. "Now *that's* a fantasy."

"And your fantasy is to play a spy," Murphy reminded him with irritation in his voice. "I'm your gadget man, remember? We're here for a spy adventure, and we paid good money for it. If you wanted to tinker around with the fem-bots, you could have just stayed as a basic resort guest without all the fantasy extras."

"Relax. I have all week to play spy games," Hunt insisted then scanned the club and witnessed the many patrons wearing official A.L.F. bracelets or watches. He grinned lustfully at each attractive woman. "Tonight, I want to play A.L.F. games."

"What about your contact? You're supposed to meet her here tonight," Murphy insisted then consulted his watch. "Actually, you're supposed to meet her in ten minutes."

A sexy woman in a revealing, red dress brushed past Hunt for her drink. She smiled seductively at him. Both noted her signature A.L.F. bracelet. She accepted her drink from the bartender and crossed the club. Hunt watched her while grinning like a schoolboy in love.

"You heard the resort manager," Hunt remarked without taking his eyes off the attractive woman so he wouldn't lose her in the crowd. "If we don't follow a clue correctly, we'll be given others." He then indicated the woman across the room with a nod. "Right now, I'm following that hot, little A.L.F."

"Come on, Hunt," Murphy groaned becoming impatient. "You're supposed to meet that woman in the alley in less than ten minutes. What about our spy duo?" His glare was demanding. "You're screwing me over here too."

"If it bothers you so much, you meet her," Hunt insisted.

"It's not my job to meet her," he remarked. "I'm not Agent Bennett, super-spy."

"Tonight, neither am I." He patted his friend on the shoulder. "Don't wait up for me," Hunt remarked then hurried across the club after the sexy A.L.F.

Murphy groaned and shook his head, obviously disgusted with his friend. While Hunt was off following his kinky inner child, Murphy was already out his first evening of their spy fantasy. He approached the bar and ordered another drink. While he waited for his drink, he allowed his attention to stray to the attractive woman dancing on stage. Ella flirted with several men while she danced, and they gave her all the attention she desired. Murphy eyed the signature A.L.F. watches the men wore and shook his head in disgust. Prostitution had never known such a high surcharge.

Shay entered the club wearing the sexy, knee-length black dress sent to her room from H.B. She wore her hair pulled back in an elegant ponytail and wore only a little makeup. A waitress discreetly slipped her a piece of paper. Shay glanced at the paper while attempting to conceal it. It read, "Back entrance. Ten minutes. H.B." Shay drew a deep breath and prepared herself for what awaited her within the alley. The intensity level of her fantasy could range from mild to wild, and she felt distrusting of everyone at that moment. There was no telling what would happen next.

Chapter Nine

Shay stood in the back doorway to the alley, scanning the entire area with apprehension. The alley was dimly lit with dumpsters and assorted trash against the walls. It wasn't one of the more glamorous sides of the resort that was certain. Perhaps it was that way by design since everything else on the resort grounds had been spotless. She didn't see anyone within the alley, but that may have been on purpose. She had no idea what to expect at this point. H.B. was her spy contact and the start of her spy fantasy. Things could turn tense any minute. She decided to play it safe and propped the back door open with an old bottle then uncertainly stepped into the alley.

Headlights from a car came on then went out in an apparent signal. Her heart was already pounding with fear and anticipation. She was now entering uncertain territory. Despite the thrill of the unknown, Shay suddenly wasn't feeling so bold. She pushed her insecure feelings aside for the sake of proceeding with her spy fantasy. She was, after all, here on a work assignment, and she needed to give her readers something exciting. She proceeded cautiously across the alley toward the expensive black car. A man got out of the car and stood in the shadows.

She strained to see his face, but he remained hidden from view on purpose, as any good spy would. "Are you H.B.?"

She then heard the sound of a gun cocking behind her. Although this was only a fantasy and not real, the sound terrified her. Shay suddenly tensed. Was H.B. just being cautious?

"Change of plans, sweetheart," a gruff male voice announced from behind her, obviously the man holding the gun. "What do I do with her, boss?"

The man by the car stepped out of the shadows. Caine Wolfe was a well-dressed man in his mid-thirties. His short brown hair was neatly trimmed, his face was clean-shaven, and his expensive suit screamed mob boss. Despite his moderately good looks, he had a sinister, creepy vibe about him. He puffed on a cigar and grinned at Shay.

"See that she's made comfortable in my car while we wait for Agent Bennett," Caine announced then looked at Shay and mocked her. "And don't forget the duct tape. We wouldn't want her screaming a warning."

Moments later, Shay's wrists were handcuffed, and her mouth was covered with duct tape to keep her quiet. She sat in the back of the expensive car alongside Caine, who seemed to study her with great interest while puffing on his cigar. Shay glanced at him periodically. She attempted to remain calm since this was obviously all part of her spy fantasy and her captors were programmed robots, but a small part of her still panicked a little. There was something sinister about the wealthy man holding her captive. Was it possible he was actually another guest? There were too many unknown factors at the moment. Caine's hired goon, Weston, remained outside the car in the shadows, leaving her alone in the car with Caine. Caine looked at his watch several times and appeared disappointed.

"Your boyfriend's running late," he informed her then fiddled with his expensive watch. He seemed to be running several options through his head.

Shay rolled her eyes at the comment and muttered something beneath the duct tape.

Caine glanced at her then grinned slyly. "Uh, oh, trouble in paradise?" he teased.

Shay glared at him and muffled something else beneath the duct tape.

"Yes, I understand every word," he remarked then grinned. "In my business, it pays to specialize in communicating through duct tape."

Shay said something else while sharply raising her brows in gesture.

Caine glared at her with disappointment. "That's rude and not very ladylike. Didn't anyone ever tell you not to piss off the man who says whether you live or die?" Caine tapped his earpiece with annoyance. "Let's go, Weston. Bennett's a no-show."

Weston immediately got into the car behind the wheel and looked into the back seat at Shay. Weston was a large man with a muscular build. He was moderately handsome despite his intimidating appearance.

"What do you want to do with her?" Weston gruffly asked.

"I can't make up my mind whether to shoot her or keep her as a trophy," Caine announced while grinning. "I'll have to give it further consideration." His look turned stern. "Drive."

Weston turned and started the car. Shay watched with some surprise as they drove down the alley and away from the club and the resort. Was this part of her spy fantasy? It didn't seem nearly as exciting as they led her to believe it would be.

"What do you think, my dear?" Caine asked while studying her. "Can you think of any reason why I should keep you alive?" He then removed the tape from her mouth.

Shay gasped with surprise then attempted to relax. "My cat will die if no one feeds him."

Caine stared at her with a bewildered look as if attempting to read into the comment. He suddenly smiled through the cigar clenched in his teeth. "Lucky for you I like cats," he teased then focused his attention on Weston in the driver's seat. "We'll hold on to her for a few days. Bennett is sure to come after her. I'm positive she has valuable information he needs."

Chapter Ten

The expensive car drove along a secluded area up a long, hilly road far from the resort then passed through the large gates to the mansion estate. The car pulled up to the impressive, two-story mansion surrounded by a tall fence meant to keep trespassers out. Nearly every light was on within the mansion as well as those on the outside, lighting the estate grounds. Caine's expensive car pulled up to the main entrance. Caine removed Shay from the back seat and directed her toward the house.

Once inside, they headed up to the second floor. Caine forced the still bound Shay into the massive, lavish bedroom. The room was furnished with an antique bedroom set, a brick fireplace, and a set of French glass doors leading to the balcony. Caine pushed her onto the bed, startling her. She was slightly apprehensive, despite knowing they couldn't possibly hurt her. She couldn't help but wonder if this was part of the fantasy or if Agent Bennett was a no-show for unknown reasons. Weston stood in the doorway and played with his gun in silent intimidation, which surprisingly worked. Shay watched both men with some nervous anxiety. Caine approached the window and opened the curtains. She saw the frosted glass with bars on the outside.

"You'll have excellent morning sunshine," he informed her. "Don't let the bars intimidate you. They're only meant to keep you in, my dear."

Caine nodded to Weston. Weston frowned and left, shutting the door behind him. She was glad the intimidating man was gone, but at the same time, she wasn't thrilled about being left alone with his boss. Again, she knew they couldn't hurt her, but that was of little comfort in her current situation. It didn't feel as if they couldn't harm her, but she supposed that was by design to make the fantasy seem more real. Caine approached Shay on the bed.

She immediately tensed and thought about everything she'd read about the A.L.F.s. What if one malfunctioned? Penny did say they monitored certain situations closely as a precaution. What if he malfunctioned and attempted to harm her? Would security even reach her in time? As Caine sat on the bed next to her, she jumped. He smiled and laughed.

"Ah, that's sweet, Caine teased. "You're afraid of me." He revealed the handcuff keys then unlocked the cuffs from her wrists. He placed the cuffs in his pocket and then met her gaze with a humored smile. "I may be a lot of things, but forcing my affections on attractive, young women isn't one of them."

Shay eyed his expensive watch and saw the stamp 'Gen X' on it. Her eyes lit with surprise. "Gen X?" she gasped.

Caine stared at her with a strange look and tilted his head. "Excuse me?"

"Uh, your watch," she immediately covered and attempted to hide her smile.

"You like that?" he asked while grinning and proudly displayed the watch. "It was a gift."

Shay stared into his blue eyes and was surprised that they weren't green like the first generation of A.L.F.s. She was also surprised he wasn't exceedingly handsome beyond compare. She thought for sure Ross would have created an Adonis as his masterpiece. Her fascination with the new Gen X had replaced any earlier concerns. Caine stared back at her, noted her fascination, and grinned playfully, catching her attention.

"Behave yourself," he teased. "You might give me the wrong impression." He stood and studied her a moment. "Sleep tight, my dear."

She watched as he casually headed for the door and left. Not surprising, she heard the door lock behind him. So Ross surprised her with his newest design, the Gen X? It suddenly made sense why his reactions were somewhat frightening to her. The Gen X was supposed to be top-of-the-line when it came to realistic responses. As she looked around the room, she realized she was officially a prisoner the rest of the night with little more to do than watch television. Somehow, she thought her evening would be a little more exciting. Apart from meeting the new Gen X model, she wasn't impressed so far.

Chapter Eleven

The lavish beachside resort was picturesque in the morning sun. The white, sandy beach was nearly empty despite the calm, crystal clear water and the warm, sunny day. Jillian followed a professionally dressed businesswoman into the elegantly decorated banquet hall. The banquet hall was already set up with tables and chairs, although the decorations and flowers weren't in place. The fully stocked bar was set to accommodate the wedding guests, and the band's equipment was already in place.

"This is where we'll be holding your reception tomorrow night," her wedding planner informed her. Trish was a tall, attractive female A.L.F. with perfectly styled hair and flawless makeup. "The decorators are coming in today to make certain everything is perfect for your reception, and the flowers will be delivered first thing tomorrow morning." She opened the double glass doors to the patio with a view of the beach just a few yards away. "And, of course, we'll be having your wedding outside. The chairs will be arranged for your guests to be seated on the patio and lawn, and the ceremony will take place on the beach as requested."

Jillian looked around while marveling at the beautiful backdrop for her wedding. "It's amazing."

"There will be room for all two hundred guests, who should be arriving today," Trish announced cheerfully. "Your rehearsal dinner is going to be in our gold room with lobster, caviar, champagne, and an open bar." Trish consulted her tablet. "You'll have a dress fitting later this morning, and we have you and your bridesmaids scheduled for spa treatments this afternoon before rehearsal. I haven't had a chance to meet your groom-to-be yet. Is he around?"

"Uh, yes, he is," Jillian announced while fidgeting. "I just haven't *seen* him yet."

The groom was the only missing piece of her wedding extravaganza. She hadn't officially met him yet, and it was obvious the suspense was killing her by the way she fidgeted.

"Sorry I'm late, darling," a man with an English accent announced from across the room.

Trish and Jillian turned and saw a handsome, well-dressed man in his early forties enter the massive ballroom. Kevin was handsome beyond all expectations. He had perfectly styled, nearly black hair and a moderately muscular body with a large, broad chest. Penny remained only a few feet behind the groom-to-be. Jillian stared at the handsome A.L.F. and appeared silently stunned. Kevin suavely captured Jillian's hands and kissed her warmly on the lips. She immediately blushed.

"You're perfect," she announced then immediately fumbled over her words. "I mean, that's perfectly all right. We were just going over the itinerary."

Jillian looked at Penny, who grinned in response. Penny was obviously pleased with their choice of groom. Kevin placed his arm around Jillian and smiled at the wedding planner.

"Are there enough flowers?" Kevin inquired. "We have to have flowers everywhere. Orchids are her favorite."

Jillian maintained her pleased smile and attempted to keep from crying. Kevin pulled her into his arms and chuckled in his throat.

"You're not supposed to start crying yet," he playfully teased.

She clung to the handsome man and eyed Penny over his shoulder. Penny grinned proudly and suggestively raised her brows. Jillian nodded her approval.

§

Suite B101. The strangely decorated playroom was filled with bizarre equipment made of leather, lace, and chains. Odd chairs, swings, and what appeared to be strange torture devices lined the walls. Round mattresses were seemingly built into the floor while things hung from the ceiling by chains. There were sex toys displayed on shelves while sexual art and images were depicted throughout the room. Mirrors were mounted on nearly every wall and across most of the ceiling. The room resembled a cross between a torture chamber and a honeymoon suite.

In the back corner of the room, Alden slept on a small mattress inside a four-by-four metal dog cage. He wore leather underwear with zippers in the front and back, and a leather dog collar containing nubs resembling spikes. Two women dressed in sexy, leather dominatrix attire entered the room. Each wore their hair in a long braid down the back, giving them an intimidating appearance. Their sexy leather outfits left little to the imagination, allowing openings for their large breasts to hang free, and slits along the middle of their leather panties. Their stiletto boots went up to their knees while fishnet stockings attached to garter belts were revealed above the boots. The first woman opened Alden's cage door and held a leather leash while the second woman kicked the cage with her stiletto boot, rattling it.

"Get up, slave," the tough woman snarled. "You have services to perform."

Alden crawled out of the cage and didn't dare look at either woman. The first woman attached the leash to his collar and pulled him across the room while the second woman lightly slapped his leather briefs with her soft, multi-tailed whip. He obediently crawled across the floor to a nearby mattress where a third woman in the same attire played with fuzzy handcuffs while waiting for him. The first two women immediately joined Alden and the third woman.

Chapter Twelve

Staging Area Three was located within the abandoned city, which could be seen beyond the resort. The abandoned city had ruined cars, mass destruction, and several dead, decaying bodies strewn along the streets and sidewalks. Becka hurried along the sidewalk with a sword in her hand. She was followed by a man carrying an ax and a woman with a machete. Dillon was possibly in his late twenties. He was built athletic and considered handsome by most standards even with his dark hair growing longer and slightly wild.

Lilly was probably only in her early twenties, although she looked older than her age. Her once attractive face was now haggard and tired. Although she kept her blonde hair pulled back in a ponytail, it wasn't nearly as neat as it probably had been before life changed for them. She wore no makeup, and her once expensive clothes had seen better days. Her hiking boots were mismatched to the rest of her attire, but there were no fashion standards in their new, lawless land. Lilly and Dillon kept close watch on the empty streets behind them while Becka kept her eyes peeled on the area before them.

"We need antibiotics for Ruben," Dillon reminded them.

"Ruben isn't going to make it, Dillon," Lilly scoffed callously.

"We don't know that," he lashed out.

"Quiet you two," Becka scolded in a hushed voice.

Becka stopped and looked around. The anxiety on her face told it all.

"Let's just get the supplies and get back to the safe house," Lilly announced.

"I heard something," Becka whispered.

"You always hear something," Lilly snapped with irritation, speaking louder than usual. "Let's go."

Lilly turned and came face-to-face with a raggedy zombie. Part of his face had been torn away revealing flesh and part of his teeth and jawbone. His dirty clothes hung on his deteriorating body, while old, dried blood indicated the action he'd seen. Lilly saw the zombie almost too late and screamed as it lunged at her. The zombie grabbed her around the shoulder and ripped flesh from her neck with his stained teeth. Blood spurted from her neck as she attempted to hit the zombie with her machete. Dillon ran to her aid and swung his ax at the zombie's head. The ax easily tore through rotted flesh, penetrating into its skull. As Dillon pulled the ax from the zombie's head, it fell lifelessly to the pavement. Lilly clutched her bleeding neck and sank to her knees. She was bleeding out fast and had little time.

Dillon hovered over the sobbing woman and looked at Becka with horror on his face. "What do we do?" he gasped.

Becka looked back at him while keeping an eye on the streets. She could hear more zombies moaning from nearby, although she couldn't see them.

"You know what to do," Becka whispered in a demanding tone.

More zombies finally spilled out from the nearby buildings, as Becka assumed they would. Their position had been given away by the noise, and they had to leave. Leaving Lilly mostly alive as zombie fodder wasn't an option and neither was attempting to take her back. Her injuries were too severe. Dillon just stared at Lilly as she sobbed and clutched her bleeding neck. Becka turned with irritation, pushed past Dillon, and without hesitation, decapitated Lilly. Dillon stared with horror as the young woman's head struck the pavement and her body twitched before falling. Becka grabbed the discarded machete, put it in Dillon's hand, and pulled on him.

"Come on!"

Dillon didn't have the stomach for what he had just witnessed but clutched the machete and ran with Becka along the street. The slow-moving zombies chased them while groaning their grisly intent. Becka opened a glass shop door. A zombie suddenly appeared in the doorway and attempted to grab her. Becka ran her sword through its mouth and out the back of its head. She placed her foot on the zombie's midsection and pulled the sword free while kicking it backward to help it off her sword. She ran into the building with Dillon directly behind her. She shut the door behind them and was immediately greeted by zombies striking the thick glass. Becka looked around the small pharmacy, which contained only a few aisles of over-the-counter drugs, bandages, and personal care items.

The pharmacist's area was sectioned off to the side by the large counter. That's where the prescription drugs were kept. Becka hurried to the pharmacy counter while Dillon stared at the zombies pawing at the door. The collection was growing to nearly a dozen. Their decaying flesh, torn, dirty clothes, and leathery skin indicated how long they'd been soulless beings. Only two looked to have turned more recently, appearing fresher. Dillon shut the blinds then turned to Becka while panting heavily, although not from exertion, and awaited further instruction.

"Grab whatever food you can stuff in your bag," Becka ordered. "I'll get the antibiotics for Ruben."

Becka leaped over the counter and scanned the shelves for what she needed. She found the antibiotics and stuffed bottles of medicine into her bag. Dillon finally came to life and packed all the food items he could find into his backpack.

"I can't believe you killed Lilly," he muttered under his breath, obviously traumatized.

"She was dead already," Becka insisted without looking back at him. "I just kept her from turning into one of them."

Dillon frowned while giving it little consideration because he knew she was right. "I know." He sank to the floor against a shelf while holding his head. "We're never getting out of this."

"Pull yourself together, Dillon."

She finished filling her bag, jumped over the counter, and approached him. He didn't get up or look at her. She couldn't babysit him. There were too many others depending on her. He needed to pull himself together, or they were all dead.

"Are you coming?" she demanded.

"I can't go on, Becka. I haven't slept in days," Dillon gasped and shook his head while trembling. "Everyone I know is dead. Now with Lilly gone, that leaves just the five of us. There were twenty of us just a week ago." He didn't bother looking up at her. "I just can't watch everyone die around me."

Becka stared at him a long moment, offered a sympathetic look, and joined him on the floor. "So you just want to give up?"

He cast a look at her, the exhaustion clearly in his eyes. "With the drugs in this place, I could end it quickly," he informed her then raised his brows. "Do you know what's worse than being eaten alive by a zombie, Becka?"

She stared at him with a curious look not knowing the answer.

"Being the last one left," he scoffed.

Becka looked from his A.L.F. signature watch to his green eyes. She offered a compassionate smile and placed her hand on his. "I'm going to get you out of this, Dillon. I won't let them get you."

Dillon smiled timidly and squeezed her hand. "I'm glad you showed up when you did, Becka. You've at least given us a little hope for the future. Any spirit the rest of us had died a long time ago."

She appeared conflicted then smiled gently and pulled her hand from his. She playfully slapped his thigh. "Come on. We have supplies to deliver. Ruben's counting on us."

Chapter Thirteen

 Shay paced the bedroom the following morning still in her dress from the club the night before. She appeared frustrated and glared at the nearly hidden camera in the corner of the room. She shook her head as if secretly signaling Ross and continued to pace. She heard the door unlock. Shay turned toward the door with growing anticipation and possible boredom. An attractive woman in her early thirties entered the room with an armful of casual clothing.

Ferrari was easily one of the most attractive women Shay had seen. She had long, silky red hair that fell just about to her bosom and a flawless complexion with just the perfect amount of painstakingly applied makeup. The woman was slender with ample cleavage and perfectly round buttocks. If Shay had to guess, Ferrari was one of Delaney's little sex-bots. She was almost positive she'd been used in numerous sexual fantasies of many guests in the past. Weston stood in the doorway and kept close watch on the situation. Given Weston's stature and moderately good looks, she could also see him being used in much the same manner. Shay wanted to stop thinking about the uses of the A.L.F.s outside their current programming. It was distracting to her situation and hard to wipe the images from her mind.

"Breakfast is in forty minutes," Ferrari announced with little emotion. "Mr. Wolfe requests your presence." She then indicated the clothing while tossing them onto the bed. "I hope the clothes fit."

"You work for him?" Shay asked.

"Yes, I'm Ferrari, his personal assistant," she informed her.

"Are you serving him willingly, or are you a prisoner too?" Shay asked.

"I assure you, I'm not a prisoner," Ferrari announced as she straightened proudly then smiled slyly. "Caine and I are in love."

"Huh?" Shay scoffed with little interest in the love lives of A.L.F.s. "Good for you."

Ferrari gave her a strange look then left the room. Weston immediately shut and locked the door behind her. Shay grabbed the clothes from the bed and looked at the camera.

"Having a blast so far, Ross," she announced then sneered. "I hope breakfast is at least good."

Shay entered the bathroom to change and slammed the door behind her.

§

Within the control room, Ross sat back in his chair while staring at the mansion's empty guest bedroom Shay once occupied and then looked at George seated alongside him.

"What the hell happened to Hunt Bennett last night?" Ross demanded.

"What didn't happen to Hunt Bennett last night?" George scoffed. "He got it on in the women's restroom at the club with one A.L.F., got hammered, and then took two other A.L.F.s back to his room. Neither of the female A.L.F.s have reported in this morning, so I'm assuming they're still with him in his room."

"It's always the quiet ones," Ross snarled while shaking his head. "Who thought this guy would be a good match for Shay anyway?"

"Don't look at me. That was Delaney's matchmaking mishap," George insisted. "Hunt came to the island a respectable businessman. Who knew he'd turn into a total horn dog?"

"Damned kids in a candy store, that's what it is," Ross launched. "I told Delaney we should make the A.L.F.s less accommodating, but he wanted his island orgy." He glared at George. "Find Penny. We need to get Hunt Bennett back on course. If he's unavailable, we'll need to reprogram one of the A.L.F.s to play the spy."

Chapter Fourteen

Shay sat at the elegant dining room table that easily seated ten guests. There were fresh flower arrangements and many fancy candles on the satin table runner. The dining room would easily fit in with any gothic fantasy. Shay wouldn't doubt they used the mansion for vampire or medieval fantasies. Again, she attempted to wipe the images from her mind. Caine sat at the head of the table with his back to the elegant, stone fireplace. Shay sat to Caine's right while Ferrari sat to his left. Caine's attractive girlfriend picked at her food and cast glares at Shay throughout breakfast.

Shay witnessed Caine eating his breakfast with little hesitation and wondered exactly how that worked. Where did the food go once it was consumed? Did his programming tell him when to eat? Did the waste self-eliminate? Or did the programmers periodically clear out the contents from wherever it was the food went? Shay noticed the looks from Ferrari and found it almost humorous that a robot could be jealous. Was it even possible? Caine sipped his orange juice and noticed the glares across the table. It was difficult to tell if he was surprised or amused.

"I'm sorry. Did I miss something here?" he finally announced noting the tension between the two women. "You two are staring at each other as if one of you stole the other's prom date."

"I don't know why you brought her here," Ferrari scoffed while sneering.

"Her date stood her up. It was the polite thing to do," Caine casually replied. "Also, if anything had happened to the poor, young woman her cat would be an orphan." His look then turned stern and almost hostile. "Although, I wasn't aware I needed your permission to abduct young women."

"Then why didn't you lock her in the basement?" Ferrari demanded.

He leaned back in his chair and casually wiped his mouth on the cloth napkin. "I'm confused, Ferrari," he announced with little emotion. "When did I put you in charge?"

Ferrari tossed down her napkin and bolted up from her chair. "I have work to do."

Shay watched her storm out of the room while Caine sipped his orange juice and appeared unaffected by the outburst. She cast a look at Caine.

"Maybe you should go after her," Shay suggested, finding it amusing that she was actually playing couples counselor to a pair of robots.

"Why would I want to do that?" he questioned while casting a curious look at her.

"Because she's obviously upset," Shay informed him and raised a demanding brow. "Judging by her reaction, she's probably going to leave you. Or, in your case, kill you in your sleep."

"Your concern is sweet, but she's not leaving my employment. She's damaged goods," he casually replied. "She'd never be able to get work anywhere, except maybe on a street corner, and with that attitude, I doubt she'd get much work there either."

Shay stared at him with surprise and near shock. "Wow, that's callous," she boldly announced. "I guess in your line of work; guys often treat their girlfriends like crap."

Caine chuckled long and hard. "Girlfriend? Is that what you took from that conversation?" he remarked then shook his head. "Oh, you're way off base, my dear." His jovial look turned stern. "She's possessive and clingy as it is. If I showed the slightest ounce of interest in her, she'd stuff my testicles in her purse."

Shay stared at him a moment with moderate confusion. "She said the two of you were in love."

"Huh?" he snorted and appeared humored. "Maybe she's a little psychotic after all."

"Not that this hasn't been fun, Mr. Wolfe, but I'm bored out of my mind," she casually informed him then looked at the camera partially hidden within the corner of the dining room. "It's time for me to leave."

Caine eyed her then gave a curious look at the camera as well. He sharply eyed her and seemed bewildered. "Who in the world are you talking to?"

§

At the same time within the resort control room, Ross and George stumbled over each other while Penny stared at the monitors and frowned.

"We should have gone with an A.L.F. on this one," Penny snapped with annoyance. "With something this important, we never should have relied on another guest with our summer attendance on the line."

"Yeah, well, talk to Delaney," Ross growled. "He thought if he could get her to fall in love, we'd get an amazing review."

"And now we're going to be crucified because of it," Penny interjected.

"I can reprogram one of our police A.L.F.s to play the spy," Ross announced while frantically pressing buttons. "It's going to take at least twelve hours to make the transfer."

"Twelve hours," Penny cried out. "We need to get her out of that house before she pulls the plug on the entire fantasy."

"He has the mansion on lockdown," George informed them. "The only way to get inside is to override the system, which means we'll have to shut down the entire program."

"So?" Penny squawked. "Do it."

"Whoa, wait a minute, Penny," Ross interjected as his eyes widened dramatically. "If we shut down the program, the A.L.F.s will reboot in startup mode. We'll have to reset the entire program, which will take an entire day. It's best if we continue with the original program using another A.L.F. as the spy."

"Twelve hours! You want her to play hostage for another twelve hours?" Penny demanded. "Where the hell is Hunt Bennett? Give me his location."

"He's still in his room with two female A.L.F.s," Ross scoffed.

"I'll talk to Delaney about it," Penny growled with disgust. "If he approves, I'm going to crash Hunt's little panty party."

Both men watched Penny storm from the room then exchanged surprised looks.

"That might be fun to watch," Ross remarked while hiding his grin.

Chapter Fifteen

Murphy rode a rented motorcycle through the small town just west of the resort. Although the town looked real, it was actually just a façade of fake building fronts. Despite what it was or wasn't, it was an amazing ride along the coast on the warm, sunny afternoon. At least the ocean view was real. The ride through the town was slightly unusual, as he seemed to reach several dead end roads leading nowhere. He was a mouse trapped in a maze. Murphy finally found the main road through the small town, which would take him back to the coast. The familiar luxury golf cart was parked alongside the curb. Delaney stood on one of the empty corners and flagged Murphy down. Murphy pulled off the street near him and turned off the motorcycle.

"What happened, Murphy?" Delaney asked while attempting to act casual, but he was obviously stressed by Hunt's disappearing act last night.

"What happened? Hunt's off banging your oversexed A.L.F.s," Murphy snapped hotly, obviously irritated himself. "The spy fantasy is officially scratched." He then eyed the town and smelled the fresh sea breeze. "I figured I'd salvage what I could by entertaining myself."

"You don't seem to share your friend's fondness for my A.L.F.s, huh?" he asked.

"No offense, Delaney, but I like women with brains in their heads," Murphy insisted. "If they can't think for themselves, what's the point?"

"It's not too late for you to take Hunt's role," Delaney informed him. "Why don't you take on the role of the spy? It'll be exciting, I promise."

"Thanks, Delaney, but I've had enough of the wonderful world of A.L.F.s," Murphy casually replied while shaking his head and sneering at the thought. "I'd rather take a ride. Maybe fish or walk the beach."

Delaney tensed slightly. "Your friend wasn't meeting an A.L.F. last night, Murphy," the owner insisted. "She's another guest playing out her own spy fantasy. A very attractive guest with plenty of brains in her head."

"Really?"

"Right now, she's locked in the mansion of an evil mastermind A.L.F. waiting for a dashing spy to come and rescue her from sheer boredom," Delaney informed him and cringed at the thought. "I'd consider it a personal favor if you stepped in for Hunt and rescued her. Maybe both of you can salvage what's left of your vacation. We could recalculate the scenario with you instead of Hunt in a matter of hours."

"Attractive, huh?"

"You forgot the 'very' part."

"Is she smart?" Murphy asked, his curiosity piqued. He then offered a grin. "Maybe a little edgy?"

"She's definitely smart," Delaney replied then considered the comment and muttered, "and by now, I'm guessing she's extremely edgy."

"Fine, I'll do it," Murphy proudly announced then grinned. "How long until you need me?"

The owner looked relieved for the first time and smiled more naturally. "Give us two hours," Delaney replied cheerfully. "Meet me back in the lounge."

"Two hours? Good; that gives me enough time to finish my self-guided tour," Murphy teased then replaced his helmet and continued his ride.

Delaney removed his radio as the smile vanished from his face. He hurried across the street to his awaiting luxury golf cart.

"Murphy's in," he announced in a gruff, angry tone into his radio. "Recalibrate the program. I want Murphy storming that mansion before sunset."

Chapter Sixteen

Caine stood behind the fully stocked game room bar and poured a drink. In addition to the sculpted mahogany bar, the game room contained a slate top pool table, several comfortable sofas, and a large, flat screen television, which took up nearly half the back wall. Caine's peaceful moment was interrupted as Weston pulled a struggling Shay into the game room. She fought against the large man while attempting to break free. Caine eyed their interaction with little emotion.

"Look what I found outside her cage," Weston announced while grinning deviously as Shay fought him. "She picked the lock on the bedroom door with a yet unidentified object."

"Oh? And where did you find her?"

"Trying to break into the trophy room gun cabinet," Weston replied.

"Hmm. That could have been messy," Caine scoffed while eyeing Shay.

Weston frowned, revealing his annoyance. "Can I kill her now?"

"Come now, Weston. Where's your sense of adventure?" Caine announced with a smile meant to mock his right-hand man. "Maybe I'll let you kill her after dinner. I'd like to see Ferrari twitch with jealousy a while longer."

"Should I lock her in one of the basement cells?" he snarled.

"Maybe it'd be more prudent to handcuff her to something," Caine remarked.

"Your call."

Weston removed a pair of handcuffs from his pocket while Caine held his hand up. Weston tossed him the cuffs. Caine caught them and approached Shay, who appeared even more agitated than she had that morning. He placed the handcuff on her wrist, smiled deviously, and cuffed the other to his wrist.

"There," Caine announced with a pleased grin. "Problem solved. Although you may be displeased when I need to use the little boy's room," he teased. He snapped his fingers to Weston, who then tossed him the keys. Caine placed the small handcuff keys down his pants, jumped slightly, and then laughed. "Oh, cold." He eyed Shay while maintaining his humor. "Come along, my dear."

As Weston left the room, Caine took Shay's hand and guided her to the bar. His hand holding hers was the first time she'd actually touched any of the A.L.F.s. She was surprised that his hand felt amazingly real, although the skin was a little softer than most man's hands.

"Can I get you a drink?"

"Sure," Shay groaned with little interest. "Why not? I may as well get plastered."

"That's the spirit!"

Shay was forced to follow Caine behind the bar. He found a bottle of wine, eyed it with approval, skillfully opened it, and then poured each a glass.

"You do that well while handcuffed," she announced almost humored

"Again, in my line of work, it's necessary to be able to do a lot while handcuffed," he teased.

He handed her one glass then took his glass and led her to the sofa. She had little choice but follow and sit alongside him. Shay sipped the wine then nodded with approval.

"That's pretty good," she informed him.

"Only the best. As you may have guessed, I'm filthy rich," he announced cheerfully. "All evil geniuses are."

Shay studied him longer than she should. She couldn't hide her fascination with the new model A.L.F. His programming was supposed to be superior to that of the older models. Where the older A.L.F.s worked on pure programming, the Gen X was supposed to think for itself. Essentially, he was a functioning laptop computer. He appeared pleased by her lengthy stare and smiled in response.

"I can't figure out if you're attracted to me or looking for a place to stick a knife," he announced while grinning with a humored look.

Shay was surprised at his ability to read her facial expressions and react appropriately even somewhat sarcastically. She then realized she had been staring, became slightly flustered, and hid her smile.

"It's a little fascinating seeing the new Gen X--" she began then immediately hesitated. "I mean, how often does a girl meet an actual evil genius?"

"And live to tell?" he joked then laughed. "Not as often as you'd think."

Shay again stared at him and studied his features. He was so insanely lifelike; it was almost frightening. Even his eyes offered no glimpse of a machine. She felt an overwhelming urge to reach out and touch him but remembered they were still living out the spy fantasy program. Maybe Ross would let her check out his Gen X in greater detail after completion of the fantasy. Caine set down his wine glass and turned to face her on the sofa while maintaining his grin.

"I like this game," he announced cheerfully.

She couldn't help but stare into his eyes, amazed at how realistic they looked. "Your eyes are blue," she commented.

He moved closer to her on the sofa. "How nice of you to notice."

Caine's sinister smile was almost boyishly playful now. He placed his hand on her leg and caressed it affectionately. Shay sprang to her feet with surprise and moved away from him until the handcuff stopped her. She'd forgotten he was a machine and not a real man. His hand on her leg felt much like every other man who'd ever felt her up. Caine smiled and pulled her back onto the sofa alongside him. Shay stared at him, knowing that look, and felt panic sweep through her for the first time.

"You have the wrong idea," she firmly announced with panic in her tone.

"I don't think I do," he replied then leaned closer and kissed her warmly on the mouth.

Surprise and anticipation shot through her entire body. His kiss was amazingly real, and for a brief moment, she almost wanted to give in to the temptation and have an A.L.F. fling. Although she didn't kiss him back, she also didn't push him away. When his kiss turned more passionate, Shay snapped out of her A.L.F. fueled sexual fantasy and immediately broke off the kiss. She placed her hand on his shoulder and held him back while staring into his blue eyes.

"I think you need to behave," she announced firmly.

She didn't want to admit what was actually going through her mind at that moment. He was warm and affectionate and already an improvement over her college ex-boyfriend. She didn't expect such affection for the character he was playing. It also didn't help that she hadn't been kissed by a man in over a year.

"I am behaving," he replied while maintaining his sly smile.

To her surprise, he pulled her into his arms and pushed her backward onto the sofa, pinning her beneath his body. He weighed surprisingly more than his size indicated he should, but his body was warm. He searched her eyes and gently caressed her face.

"You should forget about Agent Bennett," Caine informed her while smiling warmly. "He left you to fend for yourself. He doesn't deserve you."

For a moment, Shay wondered if he had conflicting programming. It was as if he was spontaneously switching personalities to match what he perceived to be the new mood. Had she caused his personality switch? Could they be so easily manipulated that they could switch from villain to lover with little more than an admiring look? It then dawned on her that his programming was more complex than that of human emotions. She suddenly wasn't sure what she was supposed to do.

Chapter Seventeen

Within the control room, Ross and George fumbled with controls and paged security while keeping an eye on the screen within the mansion game room. They helplessly watched as Shay attempted to hold Caine back while pinned beneath him on the sofa.

George pressed the intercom button and practically shouted into the microphone. "Delaney to the control room, stat!"

"What the hell is he doing?" Ross cried out while aggressively raking his fingers through his hair.

"I don't know, but stop him," George shouted and pointed demandingly at the monitor. "He shouldn't be doing that. Why is he doing that?"

"How the hell should I know?" Ross cried out. "He's forbidden to harm the guests just like the others."

Delaney hurried into the control room about to question why he was summoned when he saw what was happening on the monitor.

"Jesus, what's he doing?" Delaney cried out as he stared at the screen with horror.

"Making some serious advances on your reporter," Ross announced with concern.

"I can see that," Delaney yelled then glared at Ross. "Stop him!"

Ross frantically and repeatedly pressed a button. "I tried, but he's not responding."

"Then shut him down!" Delaney screamed.

"If I do that, he may not come back online," Ross insisted. "It could destroy the program."

"I don't care! She didn't want a romance fantasy, so she certainly doesn't want to be molested," Delaney cried out and violently slammed his fist on the desk. "Shut him down!"

Ross frowned then reluctantly typed in a code and pressed the confirm button.

§

Within the mansion game room, Shay finally managed to push Caine off her. It took some effort on her behalf and nearly exhausted her. Caine sat up and stared at her with a bewildered look.

"Did I do something wrong?" Caine asked while searching her eyes.

"You don't know?" she gasped with surprise.

"Your pulse and heart rate were elevated," he informed her. "Your pupils dilated, which indicates attraction." He tilted his head and appeared confused. "Was that--?"

Caine suddenly froze mid-sentence and seemed to stare at her.

Shay slowly sat up and stared at him with surprise. "Caine?"

When he didn't respond, she uncertainly touched him. He still didn't move or react. Shay sighed with relief then looked at the handcuff binding her to him. She then eyed his crotch and groaned.

"Oh, come on."

Shay cringed while opening his pants and reached beneath his underwear to retrieve the handcuff keys. She felt around for the keys then suddenly hesitated and raised her brows.

"Wow, that's certainly lifelike," she announced then eyed the frozen A.L.F. "Quite generous too. I guess our programmer was over-compensating for something."

She removed the keys and unlocked the handcuff from her wrist. Shay was about to stand then hesitated and checked his jacket but discovered he wasn't wearing a shoulder holster. She felt the back of his pants and frowned.

"Sure, you're the only evil genius who doesn't carry a gun," she muttered.

Shay sprang to her feet and hurried to the game room door.

Chapter Eighteen

Within the control room, Delaney leaned against the console, held his head while staring at the monitor, and groaned. "We go months without a single glitch, and the one time it really matters, you pair up a reporter with a horny A.L.F." He glared at Ross. "What the hell was he doing?"

"His programming is very complex," Ross attempted to explain.

"You call that an answer? I want security to go in there, get her out, and isolate that Gen X," Delaney launched angrily. "Either you find out what went wrong with your golden boy, or I'm putting him down."

"I don't understand what caused him to come on to her like that," George suddenly added with surprise. "That sort of response is only allowed when the guest initiates. Is it possible he could have hurt her?"

"They're programmed never to harm humans in any manner," Delaney snapped. "Besides, it's not sexually functional."

Ross appeared tense and fidgeted nervously. "Actually, he is."

Delaney suddenly glared at him. "What? Are you insane?" he cried out. "That's not something we do. We don't program our villains with sexual functions as an additional safety precaution."

"The Gen X is a prototype," Ross informed him. "I made him fully functional for every situation. He's perfect."

"*It* groped a guest," Delaney cried out. "I'd hardly call *it* perfect."

"It's just a minor glitch in his programming," Ross explained. "He's capable of every emotion and can adapt to any situation. We can use him in any fantasy in any capacity."

"Yeah, you're right," Delaney announced while nodding. "I'm seeing him as a very large can opener as we speak. Get security in there and take care of that atrocity project of yours."

Ross frowned and looked back at the screen. His expression dropped when he saw the empty sofa. Caine was gone! Horror crossed Ross' face as he stared at the vacant sofa.

"Uh, where did he go?" Ross asked.

Delaney and George looked at the empty screen as well. Both nearly lunged for the monitor.

"How did he override the shutdown command?" George cried out.

"I mean it, Ross," Delaney cried out. "Shut it down now!"

Ross frantically typed into the computer. "I'm trying, but he's not responding."

"This is an emergency," Delaney shouted. "I want you to shut down every A.L.F. in that house and send in security with cattle prods."

"That'll destroy him," Ross protested.

"That's the idea!"

Chapter Nineteen

Jillian stood before a full-length mirror within the bridal suite and admired the long, white, sequined wedding dress she wore. The dress was cut just low enough to reveal some cleavage accentuated by brilliant sequins. The train trailed halfway across the floor, although it was removable for the reception. A seamstress worked on the final alterations before Jillian's big day. There was a knock on the door, catching Jillian's attention. She looked at the door as Trish poked her head inside the room.

"Jillian, there's a young lady here to see you," Trish informed her. "She insisted."

"Uh, sure," Jillian replied, although seeming surprised. "Send her in."

Ella entered the room and marveled at Jillian in the spectacular dress. She beamed with enthusiasm. "Oh, you look beautiful."

"Ella!" Jillian cried with excitement. "I didn't think you'd show up."

"I don't have another dance set until this evening," she announced cheerfully, "so I thought I'd drop in and see how your wedding plans were going."

"I'm so glad you did," Jillian announced as she drew a deep breath. "I'm feeling a little overwhelmed."

"Well then, how about I kidnap you for a few cocktails in the lounge?" Ella announced while grinning. "You may want to change first though."

"I'd love to," the bride-to-be announced. "Give me twenty minutes."

§

Jillian and Ella sat at a small table near the window overlooking the beach. The view from the lounge was magnificent, although there didn't seem to be a bad view anywhere within the resort. The lounge was moderately empty for early afternoon. Only a dozen or more guests enjoyed a drink and the view from their small tables. Jillian and Ella talked for nearly twenty minutes while enjoying their fruity, tropical drinks.

"I've been enjoying myself so far, but I'm not sure it was worth the price of admission," Ella announced and managed a tiny grin. "I mean, it's not as if I couldn't have stayed at the resort as a regular guest and had just as much fun."

"The fantasy packages start at four times the regular vacation rate," Jillian responded while marveling at the thought. "The price goes up according to your fantasy as well."

"Tell me about it," Ella gasped. "I could have upgraded my fantasy, but I nearly choked on the price. Imagine; there are guests staying here having experiences similar to mine with full access to A.L.F. interaction paying one-quarter of what I paid. I'm just not sure it's worth it."

Jillian chuckled softly with embarrassment. "I hate to tell you what my fantasy set me back," she announced then raised her brow and fidgeted. "Take the price of an actual fairytale wedding and double that amount."

Ella nearly choked on her drink while staring at Jillian. "Are you serious?"

She nodded in response.

Ella shook her head then pushed the unpleasantness from her mind and smiled cheerfully. "Enough with the cost. Tell me about this guy you're marrying. Is he worth it?"

"Well, he's absolutely gorgeous and charming," Jillian informed her while beaming with delight. "I only got to see him for an hour earlier today before the groomsmen stole him for a round of golf."

"A.L.F.s golf?"

"I'm going to assume they go somewhere and charge," Jillian teased.

Ella laughed while grinning. "Yeah, I doubt they headed for an A.L.F. strip club." She then appeared curious. "What do you suppose that would be like?" She giggled. "Hey, baby, show me your memory card. Yeah, swing that motherboard."

Both women laughed at the silliness of the image. Jillian's smile faded, and she again appeared distracted. Ella immediately noted her look.

"Is something wrong?" Ella asked with concern. "Are you having second thoughts?"

"I'm just a little nervous about tomorrow night," Jillian replied timidly.

"Don't be," Ella announced while beaming. "I met this really cute A.L.F. last night at the club. Trust me; they're better than the real thing."

Jillian shifted uncomfortably. "There's actually a second reason for this fantasy," she announced while fidgeting. "I mean, I'm forty-five with no serious prospects. If I ever do meet someone, he's almost certainly going to have been married before. I'll never have my dream wedding." She then hesitated. "But there was an ulterior motive." She was silent a moment and appeared tense. "I've never slept with a man before."

"Never?" Ella practically gasped.

"No," she replied gently then held her breath a moment. "I wanted my first time to be special, but I wanted to wait until my wedding night. I've waited long enough. This was the only way to have my special day and night the way I've always dreamed."

"You have no reason to be nervous," Ella replied while smiling reassuringly. "It's going to be special, and it's going to be perfect."

"You really believe that?"

"Of course," Ella announced cheerfully. "A.L.F.s are designed to be great in bed. No woman out there has ever had a perfect experience her first time." She made a face. "My first time was with quick draw Stephen. He was finished before I started."

"No, I certainly don't want that," Jillian remarked and managed a smile.

"They're going to make sure your experience is perfect," Ella informed her. "It'll be wonderful, I promise."

"Thanks, Ella," Jillian replied and seemed to relax while smiling more naturally. "You'll come for the wedding, won't you?"

"Of course I will," she replied then grinned. "I'm sure there'll be some pretty hot groomsmen A.L.F.s."

Jillian grinned and laughed. "Yeah, I've seen them. They're pretty hot."

Across the lounge, Murphy entered through the main entrance and looked around. He saw Penny hurry for the beachside doors and attempted to catch up with her.

"Penny!" Murphy ran out the door and followed Penny across the patio to Delaney's awaiting golf cart. "Penny!"

Penny stopped while turning to face him then groaned and consulted her tablet. "Murphy, I'm so sorry," she announced while clearly distracted. "Things have gone a bit haywire, and we won't be able to reset the program with you as the spy."

"Oh, that's okay," Murphy replied then studied the tense look on her face. "Is something wrong?"

"Just a glitch in the program," Penny replied with defeat. "I'm afraid we've failed at a fantasy for the first time since we opened three years ago."

"Are you sure there's nothing I can do?" Murphy asked. "I mean, this is Hunt's fault, isn't it?"

"Only one very small aspect of it," she replied. "The rest can only be blamed on our programmers."

Murphy continued to stare at her and appeared concerned. "What happened?"

Penny hesitated then drew a deep, nervous breath. "The mansion where the young lady is being held was put on lockdown as part of the program, and we can't unlock it," she replied while frowning. "She's temporarily stuck inside. It's a very small glitch that's causing very big headaches for us." She again consulted her tablet. "Delaney is very sorry that you're not enjoying your fantasy vacation."

"It's not Delaney's fault," Murphy replied. "I blame my horn dog friend."

"Still, we'd like to make it up to you," Penny informed him. "Delaney has authorized me to give you a full refund and offer you a free fantasy vacation in the future."

"That's very generous of you," Murphy replied with some surprise. He hesitated a moment while she continued to sort her problems on her tablet. "I know you're busy, but I came across a barricade down one of the side streets beyond the abandoned city. It has a sign. Staging Area Three. I heard a lot of screaming." He appeared curious. "Is that normal?"

"Oh, that," Penny announced while managing a tiny laugh. "One of our guests is living out a horror fantasy. I assure you, her situation is being closely monitored, and she's perfectly safe."

"Horror fantasy, huh? That's different," he remarked. "I was just curious."

"If you're bored, your fantasy was to conclude in Staging Area Six," she informed him. "All the A.L.F.s have been shut down, but you can check it out if you'd like."

"Sounds like fun."

Delaney hurried for Penny and the golf cart. The stress was clearly showing on his face. "We need to go," he snapped and didn't even acknowledge Murphy.

Penny offered Murphy a weak smile then jumped into the cart with the anxious owner. Murphy watched the golf cart drive across the beach while kicking up sand.

A sly smile crossed his face. "But if it's all the same to you, I'd like to check out Staging Area Three," he remarked aloud to himself.

Chapter Twenty

Staging Area Three. The quiet, war-torn streets remained abandoned and nearly silent in the late afternoon. There didn't appear to be a soul around. The metal bank door gate was lowered and locked to keep the bank secure from predators. Light filtered through the front doors from the sunny afternoon partially brightening the bank lobby. The lobby had dull, marble floors, dusty chandeliers, and a long, tall cashier's desk, which could accommodate six cashiers. Becka and Dillon entered through the back and joined another woman who was tending to an injured man made comfortable on the leather sofa.

Willow kneeled over the injured man, Ruben, while the last of their group, Leon, paced the lobby with nervous anxiety. Willow was an attractive woman in her mid to late twenties, as were most A.L.F.s. Most of the resort population was attractive male and female A.L.F.s because that was what the guests wanted. Even the artificial life forms playing villains and minor roles were attractive and molded into amazing packages since they could be used in other capacities in other fantasies. Willow removed the wrap from Ruben's leg to reveal a gaping, grotesque wound that reeked of infection. Becka cringed and had to look away, but it was the smell she couldn't escape. Ross spared no details to make her fantasy seem as real as possible. Willow proceeded to clean the wound while Ruben writhed in pain.

Ruben was a bit of an A.L.F. contradiction. He was a middle-aged man. Beneath his worn and dirty surface, he would possibly play the role of a distinguished gentleman. A millionaire playboy, perhaps. Becka was deeply invested both emotionally and physically in the storyline playing out before her, so she had already forgotten those surrounding her weren't real.

"We should get out of here while we can," Leon chattered with concern.

"How?" Willow demanded and cast a glare at him. "Ruben can barely walk."

Leon shot a look at her. "I think you know the answer." He then eyed Ruben. "No offense, man."

Ruben sneered at him. "None taken."

"We're not leaving him," Willow snapped with anger. "We're safe here. If you want to leave, go."

Leon looked at the door and the horde of zombies pawing at it. "It doesn't feel safe."

Leon had managed to whine his way through the zombie apocalypse and somehow survive. Despite possibly being a handsome man beneath his weeks' worth of facial stubble, his programmed personality was offensive to the rest of the group. He wasn't a team player, and he was the only one Becka didn't trust. She didn't like him from the moment they'd first met, which was possibly by design. Every story needed someone like Leon.

"That's why we use the roof exit," Becka replied sharply, quickly losing her patience with the insufferable man.

"It's not as if there's any place else to go, Leon," Dillon informed him. "The government sealed off the city. We're stuck here. They left us to die."

"We can tunnel through the sewer system," Leon insisted.

"In the *dark* sewers?" Willow scoffed while glaring at him. "And what if they're blocked off too? Then we're trapped."

"At least I'm coming up with some sort of plan," Leon interjected.

Becka finally sprang to her feet while glaring at Leon. "You want to traipse through the sewers? Fine," she launched. "Go. I'm tired of your whining!"

"And I'm tired of you giving orders," Leon snapped. "You joined us, not the other way around."

"Well maybe when you grow a pair, we'll listen to you," Becka snarled back.

"That's it. I'm out of here," Leon shouted in anger. "You people are on your own."

"Good riddance," Ruben scoffed.

Leon stormed from the room and into the back. The others exchanged looks and shook their heads.

"You know he won't last five minutes out there alone," Willow remarked.

"It's his decision," Becka snapped.

Willow wrapped Ruben's leg with clean bandages. She had just finished when they heard a loud clunk. Becka and Dillon looked toward the back.

"What was that?" Dillon asked.

Becka and Dillon claimed their weapons and headed for the back. Several zombies headed for them.

"That son-of-a-bitch!" Becka cried out. "He let them in the back!"

Willow helped Ruben to his feet while Becka and Dillon took down the first two zombies.

"Get him to the breakroom!" Becka cried out.

Willow helped Ruben hobble in the opposite direction. Becka and Dillon continued to fight the approaching zombies while giving Willow and Ruben time to make it to the next room. More zombies poured into the lobby. Becka angrily decapitated a zombie.

"I'm going to find Leon, and I'm going to kill him!" Becka cried out with anger.

Willow and Ruben made it into the breakroom, which contained little more than a few chairs, a ratty sofa, a small kitchenette, and empty vending machines. Becka and Dillon continued to fight the approaching zombies until they were certain Willow had Ruben safely in the breakroom. They abandoned their fight and ran across the bank lobby. They slid into the breakroom and slammed the door. Willow assisted Ruben into a chair then helped Becka and Dillon barricade the door with an empty vending machine. All three backed away and stared at the vending machine blocking the door.

"So now what?" Willow gasped with alarm. "We're trapped."

They heard a faint crash from the lobby, spreading alarm through the remaining survivors.

"There must be dozens of them," Dillon announced with concern. "They'll be coming through here next."

"In a life and death situation, I'd think you people would know your escape routes," Becka remarked then pulled on a string and lowered a folding ladder from the ceiling. "There's more than one passageway leading to the roof. Go on. Up you go."

"I can't make it up that ladder," Ruben insisted while shaking his head. "Go without me."

"You can make it up there," Becka informed him. "I'm not asking you to shimmy down the fire escape, but you can stay in the attic until your leg heals. We'll bring supplies and hole up there until you're able to get around. Now let's go."

"I appreciate what you've done for me, Becka, but I'm a burden," Ruben informed her. "You have a better chance of survival without me."

"You're probably right," Becka casually replied. "And maybe we will run out on you--but not today." Her look turned cold. "Now get up that ladder, or we'll carry you up it."

Ruben hid his smile and shook his head. "You're something else, Becka." He looked at Willow. "You first."

Willow uncertainly headed up the ladder. The zombies pushed against the door and the vending machine.

"Let's go," Becka cried out while shoving Ruben's chair closer to the ladder.

Dillon and Becka helped Ruben from his chair to the ladder.

"Climb up," Dillion yelled to Becka. "You need to help pull him while I push!"

Becka nodded and climbed up the ladder. She turned at the top and reached down. Ruben painfully took a few steps up the ladder. The zombies pushed against the vending machine and began moving it. Dillon climbed up the ladder behind Ruben and helped steady him. The zombies suddenly pushed through.

Becka and Dillon screamed. "Move! Move!"

The zombies meandered for the traveling buffet climbing the ladder.

Ruben looked from the approaching zombies to Becka in the ceiling and smirked. "It's been a pleasure, Becka." Ruben pushed past Dillon and fell to the floor.

"No!" Becka cried out.

The zombies piled on top of him, allowing Dillon a chance to escape up the ladder, although he could do little more than hang on the middle rung and watch the gruesome scene. The zombies clawed and clutched Ruben's thrashing arms and legs while he put up a good fight. They tore into his flesh, ripping it from the bone with ease. His blood spilled out of several wounds, although none were severe enough to end his suffering quickly. Another zombie snarled and made its way to Dillon while Ruben screamed in agony.

"Go, damn it! Go!" Ruben cried out while the zombies tore through his flesh.

Dillon mouthed a curse then climbed the ladder and reached the top. Becka sobbed for the first time while watching the scene as Dillon pulled the ladder into the ceiling and sealed the opening.

Chapter Twenty-one

The mansion with its massive stone wall and closed gate remained on lockdown early that evening. Resort security, dressed in black uniforms containing badges, looked more like a swat team than actual security guards. Maintenance workers dressed in tan jumpsuits attempted to cut through the gate to gain access and free Shay from her luxury prison. Delaney and Penny stood by the security jeeps and watched with nervous anxiety.

The trophy room contained animal heads on the walls and their skins on the floors. Although they looked convincing, none of the heads or skins were real. There were antique weapons of every kind displayed on the walls and several weapons cabinets around the room. Shay had wedged a chair made of wood and antlers under the doorknob to keep Caine's men out, although she hadn't heard any activity since she was freed.

She frantically emptied each desk drawer onto the desktop, scattering items around and sifting through them. She finally found a set of keys and tried each of them in the gun cabinet containing handguns. She preferred handguns to the rifles in the nearby cabinet. The handguns seemed better suited for close quarters. They were the wrong keys! She tossed them aside with defeat then looked at the glass cabinet doors and realized her stupidity.

"Ah, hell."

Shay grabbed a marble paperweight and threw it through the glass on the cabinet, shielding her eyes as the glass shattered. She reached into the gun cabinet and removed an impressive .357 Magnum revolver. It weighed more than she thought possible, leaving her to believe it could be more weapon than she could handle. She sneered with irritation and a 'fuck it' attitude then reached into the case for the box of bullets. She accidentally scratched her hand on the jagged glass and immediately pulled back with pain and surprise. Shay gasped and looked at her bleeding hand.

"Son-of-a-bitch!"

She ignored her bleeding wound and concentrated on loading the gun. She didn't know how long she had knowing they heard the breaking glass. As Shay attempted to load the gun, she realized it was just a prop. She eyed the remaining guns in the cabinet. They were all props! She heard a strange scraping sound, although it didn't sound like the chair being pushed away from the door. Shay spun with concern. Caine stood behind her and removed the gun from her hand.

Shay stared at him with surprise. "How did you get in here?" she gasped.

Caine smiled as he set the gun aside and indicated an opening behind the bookcase. "Secret passageway," he announced with humor. "All evil geniuses have them."

Caine grinned slyly and took a step toward her. She held up her bleeding hand and attempted to stop his approach. He stared at her injury with genuine concern and suddenly turned maternal on her.

"You've been hurt," he announced almost as if calling a time-out.

She kept her hands out in front of her and glared at him. "You stay away from me; I mean it!"

"We need to take care of that cut," he informed her without seeming concerned with her protests.

"Don't touch me!"

"You were the one with her hand in my pants, and you're telling me not to touch you?" he boldly announced then chuckled. "That's funny."

Before she could protest, Caine grabbed her wrist and tied his expensive handkerchief around her injured hand. He held her wrist and guided her toward the secret passageway in the bookcase.

"It'll be faster if we take the secret passageway to the kitchen. We'll get you fixed up," he announced then smiled slyly. "Let Weston exhaust himself trying to break down the trophy room door. He needs to burn off some of that excess anger anyway."

Chapter Twenty-two

Shay and Caine passed through the secret passageway and into the mansion kitchen. There were rows of island counter workstations, allowing for multiple cooks and caterers. Shay counted three refrigerators, two double ovens, eight burners, and at least two pantries. She nervously sat at the main island counter while Caine retrieved the first aid kit. He delicately held her injured hand and cleaned the cut.

"It's not too deep. I could stitch it if you'd like," he informed her while attempting to cause her as little pain as possible.

"Where'd you learn first aid?" she finally asked.

"Well, in my business--"

"Yeah, I get it," Shay muttered.

Caine grinned in response then placed strips of tape across the wound to hold it in place before wrapping it securely. Shay watched him in silence as he focused on his work. He didn't look at her, but it seemed as if something was on his mind.

"Can I ask you something?" he asked, almost startling her with his politeness.

"I doubt I can stop you," she remarked while eying him suspiciously.

"Earlier, we were talking in the game room, and you suddenly disappeared," he announced then finally met her gaze with a serious look. "According to my watch, I lost five minutes. I'm sure I didn't black out." He appeared genuinely curious. "What happened? How did you do that?"

Shay stared at him with a surprised look on her face. She wasn't sure how to respond to the question. It seemed odd he'd even ask about such things.

"I, uh, don't know," she informed him. "You just sort of zoned out."

"You're not very convincing," he informed her while sharply raising his brow. "I won't be mad, but I want to know. Did you use nerve gas?"

"What?" she gasped with surprise. "No, of course not."

Caine remained puzzled and somewhat tense. "There are some men wearing security jackets attempting to break into the mansion," he informed her. "They aren't even armed, so it wouldn't be sporting to kill them. What's really troubling is that my guards are standing on the lawn like statues. They're literally frozen. Something's going on. I just want some clarity, that's all."

Shay shifted uncomfortably in her chair and realized the programmers must have done something. She didn't know the A.L.F.s had been shut down, although she did wonder why they hadn't found her in the trophy room. But if Ross shut them down, why was Caine still functioning?

"Maybe you should talk to the men at the gate," she gently informed him, attempting to approach the subject delicately.

"If they wanted to talk, they would have used the phone," he informed her. "I'm feeling very confused right now. Something's not right. I'm not even sure I know who I am."

"I thought you were Caine Wolfe, super genius," she teased, attempting to lighten the mood.

"That's evil genius, my dear," he informed her. "I'm not Wile E. Coyote." His look turned serious as he studied her. "Are you afraid of me?"

"You had me a little concerned in the game room," she reported.

"I don't get it. You should be afraid I'm going to kill you, yet we both seem to know I won't," he announced while leaning back in his chair. "It's as if I'm two different men. There's the evil genius who wants to be feared and take over the world, and then there's the man who wants to take a moonlit walk on the beach with the beautiful woman sitting before him."

She stared at him with some surprise, almost uncertain how to respond. "Wow, you're certainly a romantic at heart."

He appeared confused while studying her. "That's a good thing, right?"

"Yes, of course it is."

Shay couldn't help but stare at him. Apparently, the new Gen X had a few glitches after all. She wondered why his supposedly perfect programming didn't keep him from slipping out of evil genius mode. When Caine gently and warmly caressed her hand, she was almost stunned at the affection behind it.

"So how can I be both these men?" he asked in all seriousness.

Again, she didn't know how to respond, but she had to say something. He was obviously confused. "I think you're only one of them."

"But which one?"

"I suppose whichever one you choose to be," she replied.

"If the choice is truly mine, I know which one I'd prefer," he informed her, "but how can the choice be mine?"

Shay drew a deep breath and placed her free hand on his, catching his attention. She looked into his blue eyes. "Caine, none of this is real," Shay gently informed him. "You're not an evil genius, and you don't own this mansion."

Caine stared at her with a puzzled look. He suddenly chuckled while grinning. "We're here, aren't we?" he remarked. "It has to be real."

She shifted uncomfortably. "I doubt you're capable of understanding, but we're at an island resort that specializes in fantasy vacations," she informed him. "You're an A.L.F. That stands for artificial life form. You've been programmed to play the role of an evil genius out to capture a spy. Next week, you could be playing piano in a lounge."

Caine stared at her with an odd look. She could almost see his computerized brain attempting to process the information, which it would obviously never accomplish that task.

"What you're suggesting is physically impossible," he insisted. "A machine doesn't have feelings. Right now, I'd love nothing more than to take you upstairs and make love to you. Does that sound like a machine?"

She held her breath a moment then managed a tiny smile. "You're programmed for all those things."

Caine stared off a long moment with an almost sad look. "I don't want to believe you, but something tells me you're telling the truth." He slowly stood without making eye contact and appeared defeated. "The code to cancel the lockdown is 89043."

She watched Caine as he headed for the back kitchen stairs. Shay stood and stared after him. "Where are you going?"

"Does it matter?" he muttered then walked up the back stairs.

Chapter Twenty-three

George sat behind the monitors in the control room while watching the screen. He watched as his boss and the guards were granted access to the mansion after Shay disabled the lockdown code on the front door and the main gate. George listened from the control room monitor as Delaney and Penny talked to Shay on the mansion patio. Several security guards hurried inside with Ross bringing up the rear. Delaney attempted to fix things with the reporter who could make or break their summer season with one article.

"It was just a small malfunction," Delaney attempted to explain. "We haven't worked the bugs out of the new Gen X."

George sat back in his chair and appeared to consider something. A sly grin crossed his face as he frantically typed into the computer. Programs flew across the screen. He smiled deviously.

"And you just gave me an excellent idea, Delaney," he muttered aloud. "You want to screw my girlfriend? I'll hit the two of you where you feel it most." He chuckled evilly. "Let's see how you enjoy a little close call with our new Gen X." He pressed several buttons. "Overriding his behavior inhibitor should do nicely, and our little reporter will be there to witness it all. We'll see how attractive Penny finds you when you're financially ruined, and she no longer has her cushy job."

George pressed a button causing a signal to flash; 'Unit off-line. Not responding.'

He stared at the monitor with a slightly stunned look. "Off-line? That's impossible," George remarked. "How can the Gen X be off-line?"

He typed another code into the computer. Another signal flashed. 'All units on-line.' He grinned and pressed a button. A sign flashed. 'Confirm behavior inhibitor override.' George pressed confirm. He grinned and sat back in his chair while holding back his laugh.

"Caine and his men won't be pleased to find intruders inside the mansion," George announced with an evil, throaty chuckle.

§

Shay followed Delaney along the mansion's grand hallway made mostly of marble and wood toward the stairs just past Weston, who stood frozen while in shutdown mode. She eyed the evil man, surprised at her own feelings toward something that wasn't even real. In another fantasy, Weston could be programmed to be some woman's dream lover. Her feelings toward the inanimate object were unfounded She caught up with Delaney.

"Do you know what happened with the Gen X?" Shay asked with concern. She wasn't sure why, but she somehow felt responsible for his malfunction. Perhaps it was something she did that triggered the problem. "Can it be fixed?"

"After its malfunction, I'm not interested in fixing the Gen X," Delaney informed her in a gruff tone. "I don't need the added headache."

"You mean you're terminating him?" she asked with surprise and suddenly felt bad for Caine.

"It's not a 'him', it's an 'it'," he corrected.

Shay followed Delaney up the broad staircase to the second floor landing. Ross appeared at the top of the stairs and stared down at them.

"Well your 'it' hit the road," Ross boldly informed him.

"What?"

"He's gone," Ross remarked.

"Seal off the house," Delaney cried out with anger. "I want it found!"

He turned and headed down the stairs while Penny hurried past Weston to greet Delaney at the bottom of the staircase.

"What happened?" she demanded with concern without taking her eyes off Delaney.

"The Gen X ran away," Delaney practically shouted. "Check the kitchen!"

Penny turned and nearly collided with Weston, who now stood in front of her. He hadn't been there a moment ago. She met his gaze and realized he was staring into her eyes. He grabbed her around the neck with his arm, pulled her against him from behind, and placed his gun to her head. She screamed in response. Ross hurried down the stairs to join Delaney and Shay.

"No one moves, or the girl dies," Weston gruffly ordered.

Delaney, Ross, and Shay all stared at the unfolding scene with surprise.

"I thought they'd been shut down?" Delaney suddenly cried out.

Ross stood nearly frozen while staring at Weston where he held Penny in a threatening position. "They were," he announced nervously. He shifted his attention to Weston and held out his hands defensively. "Take it easy; no one's moving. Don't hurt the girl."

"What's wrong with you, Ross?" Delaney launched hotly. "It's a goddamned A.L.F. They can't hurt humans." He then angrily motioned to security. "Shut that thing down!"

Two resort security guards moved in with their cattle prods. Weston shot his weapon at one, but nothing happened. He appeared surprised and looked at his gun. Caine's mansion guards stormed into the foyer from outside and shot their weapons. The weapons fired, startling resort security, but they didn't inflict any damage. The mansion guards charged resort security with their rifles. Security held steady with their cattle prods.

Weston removed a knife and, without warning, slashed Penny's throat. She cried out with surprise and agony as blood spilled from the gash in her neck. He released her and took off down the hall. Delaney, Ross, and Shay stood near the bottom of the steps and stared with horror as Penny fell to the floor. Her blood spilled from her throat across the floor.

The guards attacked security using their non-functioning rifles to club them. Only one resort security guard was able to zap a mansion guard with the cattle prod. The rest of resort security was repeatedly struck with the rifles while attempting to defend themselves as they were knocked to the floor. Delaney pushed Shay up the stairs to the second floor behind Ross.

Back at the resort within the control room, George jumped up before the monitor while staring at the screen with horror.

"No! No!" He sat back down and frantically typed into the computer. "Shut down! Damn it; shut down!"

Chapter Twenty-four

The elegant wedding took place just before sunset on the beach. The patio and lawn were filled with more than two hundred neatly dressed guests. Jillian walked down the candlelit path in her lavish dress and a smile on her face. She passed Ella, who dabbed the tears from her eyes. Hunt stood alongside Ella and checked her out. Jillian approached her handsome husband-to-be and the reverend on the sand. They exchanged loving looks and smiled happily.

Once the wedding had concluded, the reception party moved into the meticulously decorated banquet hall where Jillian and Kevin danced their first dance as husband and wife as their guests watched. The banquet hall was filled with flowers on tables and along the walls. The chairs were all covered with white satin covers to match the brilliant white tablecloths. A massive buffet table overflowed with every kind of tasty treat imaginable. The wedding cake was six levels of icing flowers and sugar beads resembling jewels.

While the band played the slow song, Jillian clung to her new husband and stared into his adoring eyes while he stared back into hers. Although it wasn't actually real, it was everything she had hoped it would be, and Kevin was the perfect husband.

Jillian smiled with some embarrassment. "It's ironic," she announced. "I've been waiting for this day my entire life, but all I can think about is tonight."

"You read my mind," Kevin announced while grinning lustfully. "Want to cut out early?"

"Absolutely, but I don't think we should," she replied with some disappointment. "At least not until after we cut the cake, and I throw the bouquet."

"It's your day, darling. Whatever makes you happy," he announced. "You've waited a long time so I can wait a couple more hours."

Jillian smiled and clung to him. While most of the guests enjoyed watching the bride and groom during their first dance, Hunt led an eager Ella through a side door toward the back where they disappeared into a closet. Hunt pulled Ella into his arms and kissed her passionately and with aggression. Ella immediately returned the kiss as they wildly groped each other.

"This is so wrong," Ella announced while attempting to slip him out of his jacket.

Hunt was already pulling up her dress. "Yeah, but who cares?" he replied while grinning. "We paid a lot of money to live out our fantasies. I don't know about you, but I'm certainly living out mine."

"You're right," she announced and reached for his pants.

§

Suite B101.   Within the adult playroom, Alden was chained by his wrists and ankles to the floor bed.   He writhed around with pleasure while the three women in their leather outfits controlled his every move.   The first dominatrix lightly whipped him with her soft leather, cat-o-nine-tail as the second dominatrix straddled him while asserting her sexual dominance.   The third dominatrix was positioned between his legs and probed his body with the handle of her bullwhip.   He groaned loudly as all his senses were assaulted at once.

The first dominatrix whipped him harder.   He groaned with pleasure then suddenly yelped in surprise.   The looks on the women's faces changed from dominating to angry and hateful.   The second dominatrix dug her fingernails into his chest causing him to cry out.   Her fingernails left four long scratches across his skin, which bled freely.   Alden jerked beneath the woman and glared at her.

"Hey, not so rough!"

"Shut up, slave!" the first dominatrix snarled and whipped him harder several times, causing him to scream.

Chapter Twenty-five

Staging Area Three. Leon ran along the abandoned streets before finally reaching a large, privacy gate. The gate had been there since the beginning of the infectious outbreak, but they were never able to open it. He pulled on the gate with all his strength, but it didn't budge. It appeared to have some sort of electronic locking system. He looked at the ax he held then hacked at the electronic panel until it smoldered and unlocked the gate.

A red light flashed on top of the wall. Leon pulled the gate open the rest of the way and ran out. Murphy stood on the other side of the gate and watched Leon flee from the abandoned city. Murphy stared after the fleeing man a moment with a puzzled look then stepped into the empty street and uncertainly looked around. He heard squealing tires behind him. As Murphy turned around, several security guards leaped from their jeeps and stopped him from passing through the gate into Staging Area Three.

"I'm afraid you'll have to leave," the resort security guard announced. "We need to seal off the area."

"What's happening?" Murphy asked.

"An A.L.F. just breached the confine of the staging area," the guard replied. "A.L.F.s from this area can't filter into the general population. It'll disrupt other guests."

"Disrupt how?" Murphy questioned with some surprise while watching the guards.

Several zombies appeared from nearby buildings and headed in their direction. Murphy stared horror-struck at the meandering zombies as they groaned and stumbled toward him and the guards. Despite the knowledge that they weren't real, they were surprisingly frightening all the same.

"Yeah, I guess that would do it," Murphy remarked, unable to take his eyes off the A.L.F. zombies in gory detail.

Several resort security guards casually approached the zombies gathering on the street. They fiddled with controls on their miniature tablets and attempted to remotely shut down the robotic zombies. To their surprise, the zombies didn't stop.

"What the--?"

One guard removed his cattle prod as a second guard was tackled to the ground by a zombie A.L.F. The guard on the ground struggled to stop the attacking zombie on top of him. The zombie snarled and snapped at him with dark, stained teeth. The security guard was having a difficult time keeping the zombie from taking a chunk out of his face. As other guards attempted to intervene, they found themselves nearly surrounded. The zombie on top of the guard lunged for his neck and ripped out his throat. The guard screamed with surprise and intense pain, unable to stop the attack.

When the remaining guards saw the blood spurting from their co-worker's neck, they stared with horror and backed away from the approaching horde. The guard on the ground thrashed and screamed, drawing more attention to himself. Two more zombies dove on top of him and tore into his leg and arm. He'd already bled out and no longer thrashed Once the initial shock wore off, the remaining guards moved in with their cattle prods and attempted to ward off the horde.

"What the hell?" Murphy cried out with horror while taking a step back from the action. "That blood is real! What's going on here?"

"Get out of here!" one guard yelled at Murphy then grabbed his hand radio and shouted into it. "We need help in Staging Area Three! The area has been compromised. Send backup!"

More zombies appeared from the buildings and closed in. Murphy backed up several steps while watching the unfolding scene of carnage and horror. He was about to run back out the staging area gate when he heard a woman's shrill scream from within the abandoned city. He looked at the nearby buildings then watched as the remaining guards fought the zombie horde attempting to ambush them.

Chapter Twenty-six

Dillon and Becka attempted to slash and maim several zombies surrounding them. Willow writhed on the street clinging to her bleeding neck while coughing up blood. Becka eyed Willow several times, noting the large amount of blood pouring from her neck. There was nothing they could do for her, but she was moments away from dying and becoming a zombie herself. Dillon stabbed a zombie in the head, stopping its attack then hurried to Willow's side. Becka continued to fight her zombie, unable to get a clean shot at its head, instead slashing at its arms while it tried to grab her. She glanced alongside her and saw Dillon hovering over Willow attempting to aid the mortally wounded woman.

"Deal with her!" Becka cried out.

More zombies approached, alarming Becka. Willow's scream was the dinner bell ringing. The survivors were about to be the zombies' feast if they didn't find shelter soon.

"We have company," Dillon cried out while panicking. "We have to go!"

To Becka's horror, Dillon picked Willow up and attempted to carry her to safety.

"Dillon," Becka again screamed, now panicked. "Deal with her!"

"We can't leave her!" he yelled back and ignored her order. "Let's go!"

Becka angrily hacked off the zombie's hand then swung wildly and decapitated it. As the zombie dropped, she turned to see Dillon holding Willow.

"Drop her!"

Dillon heard her commanding words and saw the serious look in Becka's eyes. He was about to set Willow down when the profusely bleeding woman suddenly snarled and lunged for his neck, sinking her teeth into his throat. Dillon screamed and dropped Willow, as she tore a chunk from his neck. He clutched his bleeding neck and stared at Becka with horror. Becka cried out with anger, swung her sword, and in one stroke decapitated Willow. She caught her breath then looked at Dillon, who clutched his bleeding neck and stared back at her.

"I'm so sorry, Becka," he gasped while practically sobbing as he fell to his knees on the sidewalk. "I should have listened to you. I'm so sorry."

Becka sobbed softly while clinging to her blood covered sword as she stared at the fear in Dillon's eyes. She backed against the building, unable to stand, and clutched her forehead. She couldn't watch him die.

"End program!"

She shut her eyes and slowly sank down the side of the brick building while sobbing. Dillon began convulsing. Becka uncertainly looked at him as he fell to the ground and twitched violently. For a moment, she appeared stunned while watching him.

"I said, end program!" she sobbed.

Dillon stopped moving. Becka shut her eyes, held her head, and fought her tears. She needed a moment to collect her emotions. A low snarl broke the silence. Becka uncertainly lifted her head. Dillon was on his hands and knees directly before her face, snarling at her. Becka stared into his bloodshot eyes and gasped with horror. Dillon lunged at her with his teeth. She screamed and shielded her face while reaching for the discarded sword. Dillon's body suddenly jerked and jolted as smoke poured from his eyes and ears. His twitching body fell to the ground before Becka's feet. She gasped in surprise and looked up. Murphy stood over her with the security guard's cattle prod in his hand.

"We need to get out of here," he gasped.

Becka slowly stood and studied Murphy with some confusion. "You're not an A.L.F."

The zombies down the street were closing in on them. He eyed the approaching zombies and clung to his cattle prod.

"Yeah, no kidding," he snapped. "We have to go before we're an evening snack."

"Relax, genius. You just wandered in on my fantasy vacation. More like a nightmare, but it's over," she informed him then looked at the nearest camera. "End program, morons!"

"I have some really bad news for you," Murphy suddenly announced. "Your fantasy is now a reality. The A.L.F.s are malfunctioning, and they just killed several guards. We need to get out of here."

Horror crossed Becka's face. "What?" she gasped. "Are you sure?"

Murphy grabbed Becka's blood covered sword, thrust it into her hand, and picked up Dillon's discarded machete for himself.

"Yeah, we're majorly screwed," he announced. "Now let's go."

Becka looked at the approaching zombies. "Why isn't the program ending?" she gasped. "How do we shut them down?"

"Leave that to the engineers," Murphy informed her while grabbing her arm. "We just need to stay out of their path until they figure it out."

Murphy pulled Becka along the street and toward the open gate. Becka looked at the six dead guards strewn along the street in a bloody mess. Murphy grabbed a second discarded cattle prod from one of the dead guards and handed it to Becka.

"We need to seal this gate so no more get out," he informed her.

They saw a horde of zombies approaching. Becka and Murphy pushed the gate closed and manually latched it. The zombies pushed against the gate. Despite that it buckled, it seemed to hold for the moment.

"That's not going to hold," Becka gasped while staring at the gate with alarm.

"We'll block it with one of the guard's jeeps," Murphy announced.

They hurried to the first security jeep and opened the door only to discover that the keys weren't in the ignition. Obviously, the dead guards had them, and there was no chance of getting them back.

Murphy cursed under his breath and eyed Becka. "I don't suppose you know how to hotwire a car," he remarked.

She gave him a 'be real' look. There was a loud thump against the gate. The latch gave, and the gate was thrown open. A dozen or more zombies spilled out of Staging Area Three.

"The resort is a few blocks that way," Murphy informed her while watching the zombies spill out of the staging area. "I'm sure someone there will know what to do."

Becka nodded her approval to his plan, and they ran in the direction of the resort.

Chapter Twenty-seven

The wedding reception spilled over onto the patio as a few dozen guests had drinks at the outside bar. While laughing and having a good time, they heard the sound of motorcycles getting louder. A few of the guests looked around and appeared curious by the rising sound. A gang of nearly thirty bikers riding motorcycles appeared on the resort grounds in the yard and on the sand, circling the screaming, frightened guests. The scruffy, leather-clad bikers swung chains and baseball bats at the men and women, striking them as they passed. Several guests fell to the ground as the rest screamed and ran for the banquet hall.

Nearly a dozen guests ran into the banquet hall while others stood by the glass walls and stared with surprise at the horrifying scene outside. The motorcycles raced across the lawn chasing after a few guests and carelessly running over one woman. Several bikers then crashed through the glass wall into the banquet hall, driving into the crowd of wedding guests and plowing down several people. Their bodies were crushed beneath the motorcycles, spilling a green substance rather than blood. People screamed while scattering as they ran for cover. Jillian clung to Kevin with horror on her face.

The gang crashed into tables while chasing after fleeing people and struck them from behind with their chains and baseball bats. Kevin and Jillian watched several guests have their heads caved in with the wildly swinging baseball bats. Although most of the victims were A.L.F.s, some bled green while others bled red as if they were human, giving it a realistic feel. Trish ran for Kevin and Jillian. A biker rode up behind her, swung his baseball bat, and struck her in the head. As she fell to the floor twitching, he stopped his motorcycle and repeatedly struck her in the head, spilling her green blood across the floor and his bat. Jillian screamed with horror as Kevin attempted to rush her to safety.

The closet door opened to reveal Hunt with a frightened, half-dressed Ella cowering behind him. Hunt and Ella saw the mass chaos and destruction and quickly shut the door. Kevin hurried Jillian across the banquet hall, shielding her from the passing bikers. One of the gang members drove alongside them and attempted to strike them with his heavy chain. Kevin cried out with anger, caught the swinging chain, and pulled the man off his motorcycle. As the man fell, Kevin kicked him repeatedly while grunting with rage then pulled Jillian toward the broken glass doors.

Several guests followed their lead and hurried after Kevin and Jillian onto the patio just in time to see resort security guards dart past them and into the banquet hall with their cattle prods. Kevin clung to Jillian as they watched nearly a dozen security guards run into the hall after the rogue motorcycle gang.

"It's going to be okay," Kevin assured her then forced her to meet his gaze. "Lock yourself in our suite. I'm going to help them."

"Kevin, no," she cried out, refusing to release him. "Don't leave me!"

He stared into her eyes and immediately offered a gentle smile. "I'll stay by your side if that's what you want," he replied. "We'll be okay in our suite."

A woman standing next to them stared off into the near distance and appeared horrified while pointing. "What the hell is that?" she proclaimed.

The few people on the lawn looked across the beach. A horde of nearly a dozen zombies stumbled toward them, their chilling moans growing louder. Jillian stared at the strange collection of shabbily dressed people heading their way. Her eyes then widened when she realized *what* they were.

"Zombies?" she suddenly gasped with horror. "How the hell--?"

"We need to go," Kevin cried out. "Now!"

He grabbed Jillian's hand and turned her toward the resort. To their surprise, several zombies were directly in front of them, having come around the side of the building. Jillian screamed when she saw the zombie's decayed flesh festered with maggots. As the zombie attempted to grab her, Kevin pushed it away from his bride. The zombie grabbed his arm and bit him. He cried out, kicked the zombie before he could tear his flesh, and pulled Jillian for the closest entrance.

Jillian stared at Kevin's minor bite wound. It bled green as many others had. Several guests hurried after them, unable to think for themselves. A small cluster of zombies followed, although not nearly as fast. As the bride and groom disappeared inside, Murphy and Becka appeared on the lawn from the side of the building. They suddenly stopped to witness the zombies already running amuck within the resort.

"The control room," Becka cried out. "We need to get to the control room!"

"It's on the other side of the resort," Murphy informed her while nodding in the general direction.

They looked at the chilling scene within the banquet hall. Several guests lay twitching on the floor with their heads bashed in while security guards attempted to fight the armed gang members with their nearly useless cattle prods. Unfortunately, the biker's chains and baseball bats had a longer reach. It was difficult to tell the A.L.F.s from the humans since some A.L.F.s bled red as well. Becka stared helplessly at the slaughter in the reception hall.

"We can't go in there," Murphy informed her. "We won't last five minutes. We have to get to the control room and see what they're doing about this. Maybe we can help them contain it somehow. There has to be a way to remotely shut them down."

Becka nervously nodded then followed Murphy away from the chaos in the banquet hall.

Chapter Twenty-eight

The secluded mansion appeared peaceful beyond the open gates. Several vehicles were parked in the driveway in front of the mansion, but there appeared to be no movement from inside despite the open front door. Ross, Delaney, and Shay paced Caine's large master bedroom while attempting to shake what they had just witnessed a few minutes earlier.

"What the hell is going on?" Shay demanded while attempting to keep her voice down. "Did Weston really just kill Penny?" She glared at Ross. "I thought A.L.F.s couldn't harm humans?"

"They're malfunctioning," Delaney informed her then eyed Ross. "Can we contact the control room?"

"George should be monitoring everything through the security cameras," Ross assured him.

"Then why hasn't he shut them down?" Delaney demanded.

"There must be a problem."

"What about cell phones?" Shay suggested.

"We don't have cell phone reception on the island," Ross replied. "It interfered with the programs. The only wireless communication we have is the computers and tablets."

"Where's the radio?" Delaney demanded with a hint of enthusiasm.

Ross frowned. "Penny had it."

"Great, just fucking great," Delaney exclaimed then drew a deep breath and attempted to relax despite their situation. "We'll just stay here until security gets the situation under control."

"How many mansion guards?" Shay asked.

"About ten," Ross replied then eyed her suspiciously. "Why?"

"This is Caine's bedroom," Shay announced. "There should be weapons in here somewhere."

"It doesn't work that way," Ross replied. "There are only a limited number of functioning pulse guns. The rest are just props."

"So where are the functioning pulse guns?" she demanded.

"On the mansion guards for the shootout with Agent Bennett," Ross remarked.

She groaned with defeat. "There has to be something in here we can use as a weapon," Shay insisted.

"We're not going out there," Delaney informed her. "Security will contain the situation."

"And if they don't, Weston and the guards will eventually find us, break down that door, and kill us," Shay snapped.

"She's right," Ross informed his boss. "We need to get out of here and help George shut down the A.L.F.s from the control room." He eyed both and frowned. "If security didn't get a distress call out, other security officers will be ambushed by the mansion guards. They need to know the risk is real or more lives will be lost."

Shay bolted across the room and searched the dresser drawers. Ross hurried to the nightstand and routed through them as well. A bookcase near Shay moved away from the wall. Shay jumped back with surprise. A mansion guard appeared with a cattle prod in his hand. Shay shoved the bookcase into him. As the bookcase struck him, he dropped the cattle prod. She grabbed the cattle prod and ran for Delaney and Ross.

"They know we're here," Shay announced with concern. "We need to make a run for it."

Ross took the cattle prod from her and opened the bedroom door. Another mansion guard stood before the door with a gun in his hand. He pulled the trigger, but nothing happened. It was a prop! Ross zapped him with the cattle prod. The guard twitched and fell to the floor. They hurried past him into the second floor hallway. Shay and Delaney hurried after Ross carrying the cattle prod. The guards were heard running up the main stairs. Shay indicated the back stairs just down the hall. All three hurried to the back stairs and ran down them.

Ross appeared in the kitchen with Shay and Delaney behind him. The kitchen seemed oddly quiet. Shay hurried to the kitchen door and pressed a code into the pad. It flashed, 'denied'.

Shay cursed softly and looked back at the men. "I can't remember the code."

They heard the guards on the back stairs heading their way.

"Too late. We need to make it to the front door. It was already unlocked," Delaney announced and pushed Shay across the kitchen. "Let's go."

They hurried from the kitchen then crept along the grand hallway. Several resort security guards lay beaten and broken on the floor. Their weapons were gone. As they got closer to the stairs and the front door, they saw Penny on the floor in a pool of blood. Caine sat on the floor not far from her. He had his back to the wall and his head in his hands. He didn't acknowledge them as they approached on their way to the open front door. Shay hesitated while staring at him. Delaney took her hand and kept her from stopping while firmly shaking his head. Shay frowned then hurried past Penny's body near the base of the staircase. As they approached the open front door, Ferrari suddenly appeared in the doorway with a cattle prod in her hands.

"Going somewhere, princess?" Ferrari snarled then grinned at Shay.

Mansion guards hurried down the hall from the kitchen while more appeared on the staircase and ran down the steps to join them.

"Drop the weapon," Ferrari growled at Ross.

Ross appeared to consider their situation, frowned, and dropped the cattle prod. One of the guards approached and removed it.

"What should I do with them, Caine?" Ferrari called down the hall to the motionless man sitting on the floor.

Caine didn't move nor respond.

"Caine?" she again called.

Caine finally stood, straightened his jacket proudly, and walked past them to join Ferrari standing before the doorway. He looked at Delaney and Ross then stared at Shay. She stared back with concern. He eyed his guards on the stairs.

"You three make sure there aren't more intruders upstairs. Search all the rooms," Caine instructed with little emotion. As the three guards hurried back up the stairs, he looked at the guards in the hallway behind the intruders. "You four need to secure the back of the estate. Make sure we don't have any more unexpected visitors." The remaining guards hurried back toward the kitchen. Caine focused his attention on Ferrari and indicated Ross and

Delaney. "I want you to find out who these men are and what they're doing here."

Ferrari flashed a devious smile. "Do I have to ask nicely?"

"Only the first time," Caine casually replied.

Ferrari grinned her approval then indicated Shay with annoyance. "What about Snow White?"

"I'll spare her life," Caine replied then studied Shay and raised his brows. "Providing she asks nicely."

Ferrari glared her disapproval while Shay stared back at Caine. Delaney was about to protest. Shay clutched his arm, silencing him, and took a step closer to Caine. She stared into his eyes.

"I'm available for that moonlit walk on the beach," Shay announced.

Caine stared at her without emotion then removed a semiautomatic with a silencer from his shoulder holster and casually shot Ferrari in the chest. She clutched her bleeding chest with surprise and collapsed to the floor. He replaced his gun to the shoulder holster he now wore and offered a tiny smile.

"Then we should probably go," Caine informed her while suavely extending his hand.

Shay took two steps toward Caine before Ross caught her arm and stopped her.

"Is that a good idea?" Ross whispered with concern

"Better than anything you've come up with, but by all means, wait for the guards to return and kill you," Shay snapped.

She snatched Ferrari's discarded cattle prod, accepted Caine's hand, and headed out the door with him. Ross reclaimed his cattle prod and both men hurried after them.

Chapter Twenty-nine

Most of the security vehicles, as well as Caine's town car, were blocked in the driveway, and they didn't have time to search all the dead guards for the keys to the only accessible jeep at the entrance. Once the mansion guards heard a car starting, they would give chase, so the safest option was to take Delaney's golf cart back to the resort. The luxury golf cart zipped along the dark back road, traveling faster than Shay ever thought possible. As Shay watched the dark woods on either side of the secluded road, she feared an ambush at any moment, finding no comfort in the open vehicle.

Delaney drove his golf cart with Ross riding shotgun in the front while Shay and Caine rode in the back, clinging to the canopy bar for dear life. As Delaney and Ross talked quietly between themselves in the front, Caine held Shay's hand and appeared to be eavesdropping on their conversation. He leaned closer to Shay and spoke just loud enough for her to hear.

"I believe your friends intend to ambush me when we stop," Caine informed her with little emotion.

"They're a little paranoid after what happened to Penny and the resort security guards," Shay informed him. "You saved our lives. They'll just have to trust you."

"If it's all the same, I think I should disembark here and not give them the chance to fry my brains." He then eyed her with a curious look. "Or is that circuits?"

Shay didn't respond to the comment. "Stop here," she cried out.

Delaney stopped the cart, and both looked back at her with surprise to the command. Shay flashed the cattle prod in her hand, aiming it at both men in the front seat.

"I know there's been a malfunction among the A.L.F.s at the mansion, and I realize it was a serious malfunction, but Caine saved our lives," she informed them with a slight snarl in her tone. "If you boys are having any thoughts on frying his circuits or slicing open his gizmos, I'm going to be very offended." Shay pointed the cattle prod at each man while raising her brows demandingly. "Do we understand one another?"

Ross immediately nodded. "Yes, we understand."

She lowered the cattle prod and nodded. "Okay then," she replied. "Let's go."

As they resumed driving, Shay sat back in her seat alongside Caine.

Caine grinned and suavely kissed her hand. "You play dirty. I like that."

She studied him a moment then gave him a sympathetic look. "What happened at the mansion wasn't your fault," she assured him without hesitation. "It was bad programming and a God complex among engineers."

Ross glanced back at them with some disapproval to the comment.

"That you ignored your programming and chose not to harm us is nothing short of a miracle," Shay delicately explained.

The golf cart suddenly stopped, startling them. Ross and Delaney stared at the resort nearly one hundred yards ahead. Several A.L.F.s lay butchered along the ground, windows were smashed, cars demolished, and smoke billowed from a window.

"What the hell--?" Delaney gasped.

Ross stared at the destruction with horror. "The malfunction wasn't contained to the mansion."

"What does that mean?" Delaney suddenly demanded while staring at him.

"The A.L.F.s are out of our control," Ross gasped then shook his head. "I need to get to the control room and find a way to stop this."

A zombie suddenly appeared alongside the cart and bit Delaney's lower arm. Delaney cried out and pulled away before the zombie could tear through his flesh. The zombie snarled through dark, stained teeth and lunged for him. The sound of air parting was barely heard as the zombie took a bullet to the head, exploding the back of his skull, and fell to the ground. All three turned their heads and stared at Caine as he lowered his gun affixed with a silencer. He stared at the dead zombie A.L.F. on the ground with near shock then eyed both men in the front seat.

"Was that a zombie?" Caine suddenly demanded.

Shay's expression suddenly shattered. "Becka!" she cried out.

"Staging Area Three has been compromised," Ross remarked with horror in his eyes that nearly matched Shay's expression. "The zombies are loose and acting on their programming." He eyed the bite wound on Delaney's arm. "And inflicting real damage."

Caine suddenly looked at Delaney while clutching his gun. "You've been infected," he informed Delaney then raised his brows with concern. "Infection from a zombie bite is one hundred percent contagious. You're going to become one of them."

Ross looked into the back seat of the golf cart. "They aren't real zombies," he informed Caine. "They're A.L.F.s programmed to act like zombies. It's just a bite wound and probably more sanitary than an actual human bite would have been. We need to get to the control room and stop this."

They abandoned the golf cart several yards from the resort so they wouldn't be heard approaching. As they neared the resort, Shay grabbed Ross' arm.

"We need to find Becka and make sure she's okay," Shay announced with concern.

"We will. We can find her through the control room security cameras," Ross informed her. "Hopefully George already has cameras on all our guests."

All four entered the lobby and immediately stopped. There were destroyed A.L.F.s strewn across the lobby floor and more slumped over furniture. Shay noticed that some were left bloodied while others leaked a green substance. Caine studied the destruction then examined a slain A.L.F. covered in the green ooze. He appeared curious and looked at Ross.

"Why do some bleed green and others don't?" Caine asked while straightening.

"It's according to their function," Ross explained. "If we don't use them for crime fantasies, they don't need realistic blood."

"We don't have time for show and tell with the Gen X," Delaney snapped in anger while holding a cloth to his bleeding bite wound.

Caine turned away from Ross and glared at Delaney. "How about not pissing off the nice Gen X who saved your ass?" he snapped. "Don't make me regret it."

Delaney appeared surprised then looked at Ross. "Is he dangerous?"

"He's operating without restraint and outside his programming," Ross explained. "That makes him smarter than all of us combined. I strongly advise you to be polite."

Caine sneered at Delaney. "Yeah, Delaney, be polite," he snarled.

Shay took Caine's hand causing him to shift his attention from Delaney to her. He smiled and warmly caressed her hand.

"Being an evil genius has its perks," Caine informed her.

"Great, your Gen X is a horn dog," Delaney muttered to Ross. "Congratulations."

"Be happy about that," Ross remarked. "He may not have saved us otherwise."

They hurried across the lobby with Caine and Shay following just a few feet behind.

"Why did you program him to fall in love with her anyway?" Delaney demanded. "Sounds a little foolish to me."

"I didn't program him to fall in love with her," Ross remarked. "For whatever reason, he's attracted to her, and if it keeps us alive, I say let him have her."

Delaney appeared puzzled by the remark and looked back at Caine and Shay.

"If my calculations are correct," Caine informed them, "there aren't any humans among those slain."

"You can detect humans?" Shay suddenly asked.

"Now that I realize there's a difference, I'm able to read body heat signatures and organic matter," Caine replied.

"You can?" she asked with surprise. "How far can you detect organic matter and heat signatures?"

He glanced at her and raised a clever brow. "I can't see through walls if that's what you're asking," Caine replied casually. "I'm an evil genius, not Superman."

Caine suddenly removed his gun and fired past Delaney and Ross. A barely visible A.L.F. biker suddenly fell to the floor near the corner behind them. All three stared at Caine with surprise.

He eyed the three with some confusion. "What?"

Shay snorted a laugh. "You may be closer to Superman than you think."

Chapter Thirty

The closet door within the banquet hall opened cautiously with a loud creak, breaking the silence of the room. Hunt and Ella looked around with astonishment at the carnage and stared at the shocking condition of what was once an elegant wedding reception. There were dozens of slaughtered A.L.F.s strewn across the floor, most with their heads bashed in, although some appeared to have their limbs torn from their bodies. One twitched on the floor as smoke wafted from its ears.

There were few A.L.F. biker casualties, but quite a few security guards had been taken out. Nearly every table had been overturned, the wedding cake was scattered across most of the room, and the bar was reduced to a pile of lumber. Empty bottles of alcohol lay scattered throughout the room. Ironically, the A.L.F. bikers wouldn't benefit from all the booze within the bar, since they were incapable of getting drunk.

"Looks like we missed one hell of a party," Hunt muttered.

Ella cast a glare at him then resumed staring at the scene of mass carnage. "They're all A.L.F.s, aren't they?" she asked with concern for the loss of human life then nervously rubbed her chilled shoulders. The thought was frightening.

"Looks that way, although I can't be sure," Hunt replied while scanning the bodies within the disastrous banquet hall. "It's hard to tell with how realistic they'd created the A.L.F.s."

"I think you, Jillian, and I were the only humans at this wedding," she remarked then scanned the bodies as well and grimaced. She spun to face Hunt. "We need to find Jillian."

"How?" he demanded while looking back at her with surprise.

"I don't know," Ella replied nervously and shook her head as she again scanned the room. "I guess we should look around the resort."

They heard a low groan that caused them to freeze. Both uncertainly looked across the ruined wedding venue. Two zombies stained with blood and green substance entered through the broken glass. One zombie had the entire side of its face torn off, exposing flesh and bone. The other zombie was missing its arm from the elbow down.

"You can look around," Hunt suddenly announced. "I'm keeping my ass in the closet."

She glared at him with annoyance. "What was your fantasy? To grow a pair?"

Ella hurried across the ballroom, stepped over several disabled A.L.F.s, and snatched a blood-soaked baseball bat. The zombies spotted her and headed in her direction.

More entered the ballroom, saw Hunt by the closet, and headed for him as well. It was too late. He'd been seen.

Hunt groaned and hurried after Ella. "Wait! I'm coming with you!"

Chapter Thirty-one

Kevin and Jillian bolted through the basement door and stopped on the landing just before the carpeted stairs. Kevin locked the door behind them and stepped away from it. There was thumping against the door as someone attempted to enter. Kevin looked at Jillian in her dirty, torn wedding dress.

"They're going to get through that door," Kevin informed her. "We need to see if there's somewhere else down here to barricade ourselves until security can contain the problem."

Jillian nervously nodded and uncertainly walked down the steps while holding her long dress. Kevin remained close behind her. They entered the basement hallway and saw suite doors on either side of the corridor. Their placement seemed unusual, considering the luxuriousness of the resort.

"These look like suites," Jillian informed him with some surprise.

"Who'd put suites in a basement?" Kevin asked and appeared puzzled.

Jillian uncertainly shook her head as they approached one of the two suite doors, Suite B101. Kevin tried the door. It was unlocked. He opened the door and cautiously entered. Jillian followed Kevin into the massive, dimly lit suite. He immediately locked and bolted the door behind them then took a closer look around. Through the dim lighting, they realized the room was designed for some sort of sexual bondage fantasy.

"Talk about bizarre," Kevin muttered then looked around. "We need to barricade the door." He indicated the strange sofa. "That should do."

Jillian looked past the sofa and deeper into the darkened room. Her expression immediately dropped, and she uncertainly crossed the suite. Kevin stared at her with concern.

"What is it?"

"I'm not sure--"

Jillian suddenly stopped, appeared horrified, and let out a scream. Kevin hurried to her side. A naked and restrained Alden lay on the bed with most of his flesh whipped from his body. Jillian clung to Kevin and buried her face into his shoulder.

"What the hell happened to him?" Kevin gasped.

They heard a whip crack. Both suddenly looked across the room. The three women in their bloodied leather outfits held their cat-o-nine tail and bullwhip, which still contained particles of flesh and blood. They grinned and approached the bride and groom.

"Oh--" Kevin muttered with concern while staring at the frightening women with blood spattered on their bare arms and legs.

Jillian clutched his arm. "We need to get out of here."

Kevin pulled her toward the door. The three women bolted after them. One cut off their path while the other two grabbed Kevin.

The first dominatrix eyed him while grinning lustfully. "Oh, he'll do."

The dominatrix by the door grabbed Jillian by her hair and pulled it, causing her to scream. "I got the princess. She's mine."

"No! No!" Jillian cried out.

"Let her go!" Kevin shouted while fighting against the two women holding him captive.

The first woman punched Kevin in the crotch and sent him to his knees. He clutched himself, apparently a programmed response to the assault.

"I think you should worry more about what we're going to do to you, slave," the second woman snarled at him.

"No," Jillian cried out in anger. "This is my wedding day!"

Jillian rammed her high heel into the top of the woman's bare foot, puncturing her flesh and bone. As the dominatrix cried out, Jillian rammed her elbow into her abdomen then spun and punched her in the face. She grabbed the bullwhip from her, turned, and cracked it at one of the women holding Kevin. It caught her booted ankle. Jillian yanked back and pulled her foot out from under her. Kevin recovered, sprang to his feet, and punched the remaining woman alongside him. She appeared almost unaffected, grinned, and punched him back. He was somehow unaffected by the hit then punched her repeatedly until she fell.

As the fallen woman began to stand, Jillian approached and stomped on her face with her high heel, stabbing her through the eye. Jillian spun toward the woman clutching the wound on her foot and glared at her. She held her hand up and moved away from the door. Jillian and Kevin darted from the room and hurried into the corridor. They heard a loud crack at the top of the steps. Both looked up the stairs. Although they couldn't see much in the dim lighting, they could hear mass movement on the steps, indicating their attackers had gotten through the upstairs door.

The distinct sound of chains rattling horrified them. The couple ran to the door across the hall and attempted to open it. It was locked. Kevin struck it several times with his shoulder. On the third attempt, it broke open. Both hurried inside and shut the door behind them. Kevin leaned against the door while Jillian placed the deadbolt across it. Thankfully, it held. She turned on the light to reveal a similar playroom.

"Oh, crap," she gasped while nervously running her fingers through her hair.

They grabbed the sofa and pushed it against the door. There was pounding from outside the door. It moved slightly but didn't give. Both backed away from the door and scanned the bondage room. Thankfully, it wasn't occupied.

"We'll block the door with a few more items and hopefully keep them out until help arrives," Kevin announced reassuringly.

Once they had the door barricaded with the sofa and several heavy items piled on top of it, Jillian and Kevin stood back and stared at the barricade. They could still hear pounding, but the door no longer moved.

"I think we're safe for a while," Kevin reassured her. "Hopefully they'll get bored when they realize they can't get in and leave."

Jillian stared at the door with concern and fright then looked at Kevin. "Promise you won't let them touch me," she practically gasped.

Kevin looked at Jillian then pulled her into his arms and held her. "I promise I won't let them touch you," he whispered into her ear.

She pulled back and met his gaze. Kevin offered a sympathetic smile and wiped the dirt from her face.

"I'm so sorry, darling," he announced with amazing tenderness. "I wanted this day to be special for you. Now it's ruined."

She attempted a smile. "It can still be special."

Kevin stared at her a moment then kissed her warmly. She returned the kiss with a little more passion.

Chapter Thirty-two

Caine and Shay followed Delaney and Ross along the business office corridor toward the west wing of the resort. Although there appeared to be no damage, the wing was eerily silent and void of employees.

Caine suddenly stopped and looked around. "I smell smoke," he announced.

Shay pulled him along to keep up with the men. All four slowed when they saw smoke in the corridor coming from the room just ahead.

Ross appeared horrified and screamed, "No! No!"

He ran for the door and pushed it open. Smoke billowed out as the sprinklers attempted to contain the remaining fire. Ross shut the door and appeared shocked while shaking his hand, having burned it on the hot doorknob.

"It's gone," Ross gasped and sank against the hall wall. "It's all gone."

"George?" Delaney asked.

"I didn't see any bodies, so George must have gotten out."

"Is there any other way to shut down the rogue A.L.F.s?" Delaney asked.

"Whatever caused the incident at the mansion must've caused all the A.L.F.s to malfunction," Ross insisted. "They stopped responding to the deactivation order, perhaps because of whatever caused the fire in the control room."

"Arson," Caine informed him.

All three looked at Caine.

"Excuse me?" Delaney demanded.

"I smell kerosene," Caine replied. "That fire was intentionally set."

"The rogue A.L.F.s?" Ross gasped with surprise.

"Do A.L.F.s think outside their programming?" Caine asked. "Would they rationalize their mortality depends on destroying this room?" He raised his brows. "Even I didn't know that until you told me."

"No, the A.L.F.s are operating on their current programming," Ross remarked. "If they're programmed for violence, they'll act out violently."

"So only a human would have reason to destroy the control room," Caine deducted.

Delaney and Ross exchanged stunned looks and immediately came to the same conclusion.

"George?" Delaney gasped. "Why?"

"Is George a programming genius?" Caine asked.

Ross nodded.

"Then as a computer genius yourself, you tell me," Caine asked with a curious look. "Why would *you* need to destroy the control room?"

Ross considered the question then stared at Caine with wide, horrified eyes. "To cover up what I did." He then looked at Delaney. "George altered the A.L.F.s programming. He stripped away their restraints to harm humans sending them on a rampage."

"But why?" Delaney demanded.

Ross stared at him and frowned. "To get back at you."

"Me?"

"For stealing Penny from him."

Delaney was only momentarily surprised by the comment then turned angry. "For that, he'd destroy billions of dollars in property and allow the deaths of countless humans?" he cried out. "Penny's dead because of him."

"That wasn't his intent. I doubt he thought it'd go this far," Ross informed him. "George is not a killer, but he is a hotheaded idiot."

"Great, now what?" Shay scoffed.

"There has to be another way to shut down the A.L.F.s," Delaney demanded.

Ross shook his head. "No, there's--" His eyes suddenly lit up. "Wait! There's the tower satellite. If we disable it, all the A.L.F.s will shut down."

"Are you sure?" Delaney asked with enthusiasm.

"Absolutely," Ross replied. "We just need to put in the code, and it'll shut down. Almost as easy as flipping a light switch."

"What about Caine?" Shay asked.

"It's just a shutdown. Once we have the rogue A.L.F.s, we can shut them down permanently and then reboot the system," Ross replied. "The rest of the A.L.F.s will reboot in their current programming. I assure you, he'll be fine."

"Until you pull his plug after he's shutdown," Shay demanded while folding her arms across her chest.

"I won't do that," Ross insisted.

"We don't know how many guests and staff have been killed, Shay," Delaney informed her. "They're far more important than one A.L.F."

"It'll be okay, Shay," Ross assured her. "You can stay by Caine's side and make sure we don't disable him."

Shay glanced at Caine.

He offered a tiny smile and shrugged. "I trust you, Shay."

"Isn't that tower part of the old lighthouse?" Delaney asked. "That's one hell of a hike."

"It's not that far," Ross informed him. "It's just a few miles past the mansion."

"Isn't there a self-destruct fail-safe at the satellite?" Delaney asked.

"Yes, it can be blown on-site with a code, but then you'd lose every A.L.F. at the resort," Ross informed him. "It would destroy the server, their programming, and just about every electronic resort function. The fail-safe was designed to destroy the A.L.F.s in the event of a major malfunction."

Delaney appeared to consider the idea then shook his head. "No, we should salvage what we can with the shutdown," Delaney muttered. "We've lost enough already."

"Stupid question," Caine announced while raising his finger in gesture. "If this programmer of yours caused all this and started this fire to keep anyone from tracing the destruction back to him, why would he run?"

Delaney and Ross exchanged looks. Both appeared horrified and cried in unison, "The tower!"

"He knows if he blows the tower, it'll stop the destruction," Ross announced, "but it'll also help cover his involvement."

"We need to get there before he does," Shay announced.

"He's had a healthy head start," Ross grumbled.

"Then I guess we'd better go fast," Caine remarked.

"George would have taken a golf cart up the main road," Ross announced. "If we can get a jeep up the shorter, rockier pass, we may be able to get there before him."

Delaney cast a look at Shay. "You should probably stay here," he insisted. "The security office is just down the hall. You can lock yourself inside."

"What about Becka?" she asked.

"There are monitors in the security office," Ross informed her. "You'll be able to search the grounds via video feed for her."

"Under no circumstances are you to go after her," Delaney firmly warned. "If you find her, you radio security."

"Is anyone in security still alive?" Shay asked with concern.

"You can radio them and find out," Delaney replied. "Just don't come out of that security office." He cast a sharp glare at Caine. "And don't let the Gen X touch anything."

Caine sneered at Delaney. "I'm developing a healthy dislike for you, Delaney," he snapped. "You better hope I never have to save your life again, because I probably won't."

Chapter Thirty-three

There was violent pounding against the door to Suite B102. The furniture piled against the door moved with each vibration. With the next thrust, the furniture was thrown from the door, and several biker A.L.F.s spilled into the room with their bloodied baseball bats and chains. They fanned out and searched the room like a bunch of crazed maniacs. The first biker reached the bed at the far end, which contained a mass under the covers. He raised his baseball bat prepared to strike the huddling couple then hesitated and stared a moment.

Jillian and Kevin were naked beneath the covers locked in a lover's embrace. Jillian's eyes were open and fixated on nothing. Blood was visible on the corner of her mouth, and there were deep black and blue marks from a man's hand on her throat. A green substance soaked through the sheets. The biker A.L.F. appeared curious and pulled the covers back to reveal the deep, jagged cut along Kevin's wrist, and the broken metal still clutched in his hand. He'd kept his promise to the woman he'd loved.

§

Ella hurried across the battlefield that was once the lobby while carrying the baseball bat she'd found. Hunt hurried after her and followed her to the front desk. Ella ran behind the desk and removed a master key card.

"Maybe we should try the phones again."

"The phone in the banquet hall didn't work, so this one won't either," Ella informed him. "Those bikers must have destroyed the phone lines."

"What makes you think she's in the honeymoon suite?" Hunt asked.

Ella hurried out from behind the desk and didn't bother looking at Hunt. "She was looking forward to her wedding night," she replied. "I'm hoping they left the reception early, avoiding all this. If they did, that's where they'd go."

"Well, the honeymoon suite is as good a place as any to hide until this blows over," Hunt remarked. "Sounds like a solid plan to me."

They hurried for the elevators while avoiding the massive amount of blood and flesh strewn across the lobby. They finally reached the elevator, pressed the button, and kept watch on the area around them to avoid any surprise attacks by the A.L.F. bikers. When the elevator dinged, both turned as the doors opened. Several zombies stood in the elevator, flesh hanging from their stained teeth and blood dripping from their chins. Ella and Hunt saw blood painting the walls and floor leading down to a partially eaten human employee on the elevator floor.

The sight of the dead woman was particularly traumatizing. The poor, unfortunate woman had met with a grisly death, having her insides torn from her body, leaving her hollowed and discarded on the floor. Considering there were no marks on her neck and throat, there was a strong reason to believe she was still alive when they tore her insides out.

The zombies lunged for Ella and Hunt. Ella screamed and swung the baseball bat while Hunt took off across the lobby. Ella saw him running and attempted to flee as well after striking the zombies with the bat. The moment she attempted to turn, they swarmed her, clawing and biting her arms. She attempted to fight them while screaming and swinging the bat despite the flesh they were tearing from her. All four zombies finally threw her off balance and tackled her to the floor. One dove for her midsection and immediately tore into her abdomen while another ripped into her face. The other two grabbed her legs and tore into her flesh with their teeth while she screamed.

Chapter Thirty-four

Shay and Caine looked around the abandoned security office, which seemed secure at the moment. The heavy doors and thick locks were all they needed to keep out unwanted visitors. Shay checked the security camera monitors and immediately fiddled with them, attempting to figure out how to switch locations and pan the camera in different directions. Caine approached a nearby computer and played on it. Shay glanced at him, curious to see what he was doing. He typed on the keyboard with lightning speed, allowing programs to flash on the monitor then disappear as if by magic. Shay wondered if he was that smart or if it just appeared that way. What was he possibly looking for?

"Are you actually reading that fast?" she finally asked him.

"Did you know Ross' password is Ross#1?" he asked without looking at her then shook his head. "Kind of sloppy for a programming genius." He was silent a brief moment. "I made it into the control room computer system."

"I thought the computer was destroyed in the fire," Shay remarked while turning on her chair to face him.

"Hard drive is still intact," he informed her. "The server is allowing me to access the hard drive."

She stared at him with surprise. "Can you shut down the A.L.F.s?"

"No, that program has been corrupted," he informed her. "It would seem George slipped into the mainframe to remove the security settings for the A.L.F.s at the mansion, but inadvertently stripped the entire resort." He shook his head and snorted with disgust. "He must have realized his mistake, and in his haste to fix it, he incorrectly coded it. All of this is easily traced back to him, so he felt the need to destroy the main computer system."

"So we can't stop this from here?" she asked, feeling her entire body sag with defeat.

"No. I could crash the system, but that would wipe out all the A.L.F.s," he informed her. "They'll disconnect from the server, shut down, and fry their circuits when they reboot."

Shay stared at him with some surprise. That would destroy every A.L.F. at the resort, including Caine.

"We'll have to trust that Ross can shut down the system without crashing it," Shay announced, although the thought concerned her.

Caine cast a look at her and smiled almost boyishly. "You just don't want to see my brains fry," he teased playfully. "You like me, admit it."

She hid her smile. "Yes, I like you, Caine."

He sat back in his chair and stared at her with a strange, solemn look on his face. "They're going to disable me, aren't they?" he asked with defeat in his tone. "Once they shut down the system, I'm going to go offline, and you're not going to be able to stop them from destroying me."

Her body immediately tensed as she stared at him. "I'm not going to let that happen."

"I believe you'll try, but Delaney isn't going to allow me free will," he firmly insisted. "After the A.L.F.s malfunction, he's going to err on the side of caution and put me down too."

"You underestimate me and my reporter status," she announced boldly. "Is there any way to keep you from shutting down with the rest of the A.L.F.s?"

Caine returned to the computer and speed typed. He remained focused on the screens flying past then suddenly stopped.

"I found the programming for the A.L.F.s as well as myself, the Gen X." He frowned and shook his head. "I don't see any way to separate myself safely from the server. I'll be shut down with the others." Caine leaned back in the chair and stared at the computer with disgust. "I'm completely at their mercy."

Shay frowned, approached him, and sat on the arm of his chair. She placed her arms around his neck and clung to him.

"I'll do everything I can, Caine," she gently replied. "I promise."

Caine pulled her onto his lap, surprising her, and gently touched her face while smiling. "I trust you to do your best, Shay."

Shay stared into his eyes a moment then kissed him warmly on the lips. Caine immediately returned the kiss then pulled away before it became too aggressive.

"There's something I'd like to do before I'm shut down," he informed her.

Shay blushed and hid her smile. "I'm not sure this is the best place for that, but I won't deny your request."

He stared at her with some surprise. "Wow, I really appreciate that," Caine announced then chuckled, "but I meant I wanted to help you find your friend."

Shay felt her cheeks redden as she shifted with embarrassment. "Oh."

He then grinned, mocking her. "We can do the other thing later."

"If she's hiding, we're going to have a hard time finding her with the security cameras," Shay remarked and struggled to move from his lap, which he was reluctant to release her.

When she finally broke free, Caine resumed working on the computer.

"With Ross' passcode; I can link the security cameras to the resort cameras, which can identify humans by their body heat." He cast a look at her and grinned deviously. "In ten minutes, we'll know where every live human is within two miles."

Shay sprang alongside his chair and stared at the monitor with enthusiasm. "By all means, link them."

Caine typed frantically into the computer. The security cameras switched and repositioned. Shay moved to the monitors and watched closely.

"It's not picking up much," she remarked with concern. "Are they all dead?"

"The computer indicates there are twenty-two viable humans," he responded.

"Viable?"

Caine cast a look at her and raised his brows. "Still giving off body heat."

"Twenty-two?" she gasped and felt her heart sink. "Out of nearly three hundred humans, you're telling me there are only twenty-two left breathing?"

"Within a two-mile radius, yes," he replied. "Perhaps some escaped on boats."

"Let's hope so."

Shay continued to watch the cameras. They could see several images of those locked within rooms. Most appeared safe for the moment. She then saw an image of Becka on the screen.

"There! That's her," she cried out. "She's alive! Pan back. Get a fix on her location."

Caine stared at the screen, sat back in the chair, and frowned. "I don't have to," he muttered with disgust. "That's my mansion."

Chapter Thirty-five

Murphy kept watch on the hallway while Becka kneeled over Penny's blood-soaked body where it remained in the hallway near the stairs. She then checked the resort security guards even though she was almost certain they were all dead. She grimaced at the way they must have died, having been beaten to death. Whatever happened to them, it appeared they didn't have much of a fighting chance. Becka finally straightened and nervously looked around the hallway strewn with dead bodies.

"Are you sure this is where Delaney wanted you to meet him?" she asked with concern, not seeing Delaney's body among those killed.

"Yes, he needed me to fill in for Hunt," Murphy informed her. "He was supposed to meet a woman in the alley outside Club A.L.F. but got caught up in his own sexual fantasies instead." Murphy appeared curious. "The abducted woman was your friend?"

"Is," she corrected then stared at him with a look of fear on her face. "I know she's alive somewhere. We need to find her, Murphy."

"This place is huge."

"I don't care," Becka announced proudly, acting braver than she was. "She'd look for me."

Murphy placed his hand on her shoulder and stared into her eyes. "We'll find her, Becka," he insisted. "I wasn't suggesting we give up and hide. It's just--this place is massive. It's going to take a while to search it."

She attempted to relax while trembling. "I'm sorry," she muttered. "It's been a rough week."

"This level seems pretty quiet," he informed her then glanced up the staircase. "Let's start upstairs and work our way down. If she's hiding somewhere, I'd suspect she'd be in one of the bedrooms, since they have locks on the doors." He gave her a stern look. "We'll go slow and quiet."

Becka nodded in response. They were heading up the broad staircase when they heard movement from the second floor. Both immediately stopped and stared at the floor above them. Mansion guards with cattle prods appeared at the top of the steps. Becka and Murphy quickly turned to head back down the steps. More mansion guards appeared at the bottom of the steps, blocking their escape. Weston stepped out from one of the rooms on the first floor and smiled at them.

"Welcome to Wolfe Manor," he announced while grinning deviously. "Please put your weapons down. Don't make me ask twice."

Becka and Murphy uncertainly set their weapons down. The mansion guards forced them down the stairs to join Weston among the dead bodies.

Weston approached them and grinned, apparently pleased. "So, you came here looking for Agent Bennett's girlfriend. That means he can't be far behind." He then eyed the guards. "Lock them in the dungeon cell. We need them alive."

The guards forced them along the hallway toward the kitchen with the cattle prods dangerously close to their backs.

Murphy eyed Becka as something dawned on him. "They're still running on their original programming," he whispered with surprise. "We could get out of this alive if we play along."

"Unfortunately, that also means we need Agent Bennett to show up and save us," Becka muttered back while meeting his gaze. "What are the chances of that happening?"

He frowned with disappointment. "Don't hold your breath," he remarked. "If I know Hunt, he's probably hiding in a closet somewhere."

"I'm glad you still have a sense of humor," she muttered.

Murphy snorted a laugh while looking away. "Yeah, I wish I were joking."

Chapter Thirty-six

Shay drove the jeep along the back road while Caine continued working on a resort tablet. Shay glanced at him several times.

"Where did you get that?"

"From the dead woman back at the mansion," he casually informed her. "I have amazingly spacious inner jacket pockets."

"That's Penny's tablet?" she practically gasped. "What are you doing with it?"

"What evil geniuses do best," he informed her. "Stacking the deck in my favor."

"How can Penny's tablet help?"

"It's one of the few electronic devices on the island equipped with a wireless connection," he announced while glancing at her. "I've tapped into the server in the security office, which is connected to the server from the control room. It gives me access to the entire resort."

"Access?" she asked with surprise while casting a look at him. "What sort of access?"

"Everything from turning on the kitchen lights to reprogramming the A.L.F.s," he announced without looking up from the device.

Shay suddenly stopped the jeep, jerking both in their seats and turned to face him with surprise. "You can control the A.L.F.s."

"No, I said it'll give me access," he corrected her. "It's a very complex program, even for an evil genius." He stared into her eyes with a serious look. "I know you'd like it if I could shut down the A.L.F.s, but your friend may not have a lot of time. I suggest you keep driving."

Shay stepped on the gas, nearly burning out on the back road. "I hope she's okay."

"They're detaining her in the dungeon cells with another human male," Caine informed her.

"How can you possibly know that?"

"I'm also equipped with a wireless connection," he casually replied. "I just finished downloading the system's camera feeds into my memory."

She eyed him with surprise. "You mean you can see what the security cameras see?"

"Actually, I'm controlling the security cameras," he informed her then grinned. "It's like seeing the resort through hundreds of eyes. Very fascinating." His look then turned serious. "Watch out for Agent Bennett fifty yards in front of us."

Shay appeared bewildered then looked back at the road. She saw Hunt suddenly appear in front of her while frantically waving his arms. Shay slammed on the brakes to avoid hitting him. Hunt hurried for the jeep and jumped into the back.

"I don't have time to explain," Hunt gasped while out of breath. "You have to turn around. This road isn't safe."

"We have to get to the mansion just up the road," Shay informed him. Ironically, there wasn't any safe place left on the island.

"No, you can't go there. That place is crawling with A.L.F.s," Hunt informed them. "I was in a jeep with Delaney and one of his programmers when they ambushed us."

"Delaney?" she gasped and stared at him with surprise. "What happened to them?"

"The rogue A.L.F.s seemed interested in taking them alive," Hunt informed her while panting out of breath. "I took off before they could capture me too."

"They're locking them in one of the cells in the dungeon," Caine informed her then raised his brows. "Delaney has been wounded."

Hunt stared at Caine's profile. "How did you--?" Horror suddenly crossed his face, and he wildly gestured. "Oh, my God! You're an A.L.F.!"

Caine cast a casual look at Hunt in the back. "No, I'm a Gen X."

Hunt gave Shay a bewildered look.

She smirked, humored by his confusion. "It means he's evolved," she replied. "Don't worry; he no longer wants to hurt you."

"What do you mean 'no longer'?"

"Apparently, you were supposed to play the role of a spy and Caine was your adversary," Shay informed him then smirked. "You were also supposed to rescue me but never bothered to show. I'll thank you for that later."

Caine eyed Hunt and smiled slyly. "It's best that you were a no-show. You didn't stand a chance against me. It would have been a slaughter." He then glanced at Shay and grinned. "You're better off with me, my dear."

Shay smiled gently then appeared more serious. "What are we going to do about Becka?"

"Obviously, we're going to rescue her," Caine replied simply.

"How?"

"Are you out of your mind?" Hunt practically gasped and squirmed in his seat.

Caine cast a chilling glare at Hunt in the back seat. "You can get out right here, Agent Bennett. No one's asking you to go along." He cast a look at Shay and shook his head. "You are *so* much better off with me." He glared back at Hunt. "In or out. We're on a tight schedule."

Hunt frowned and reluctantly got out of the jeep. Shay burned out on the road as she pulled away from Hunt. Caine continued to fiddle with the tablet.

"What a jerk," Shay scoffed and resumed concentrating on her driving.

"Were you aware that Delaney thought you and Hunt Bennett would hit it off?" Caine announced while scanning the tablet. "He thought you'd make a great couple. Supposedly, Hunt is a fine catch."

"That figures," she snapped. "I specifically told him I didn't want the romance package."

"What's wrong with romance?"

"There was this guy in college," Shay reluctantly informed him then frowned at the thought. "He sort of ripped out my heart and stomped on it."

"He's obviously a fool."

Shay glanced at Caine and the smile on his face. She hid her smile and focused on her driving.

Caine finally set the tablet aside and indicated the dark road before them. "Pull over up here," he announced. "I'll walk the rest of the way."

Shay pulled off the road and looked at him. "You mean *we'll* walk the rest of the way."

"No, it's too dangerous for you to go anywhere near my mansion," he informed her then handed her the tablet. "I'll communicate with you through this."

"You can't go alone," she protested.

"Sure, I can. It's my mansion. They're my men," he replied simply and smiled charmingly. "I'll walk right through the front door larger than life."

"What if you took me as your prisoner?" she suggested. "Tell Weston you captured me."

Caine studied her a long moment then frowned. "It might work, but I'd rather not risk it."

"We know the specially made resort guns work on the A.L.F.s," she informed him.

"Yes, they're magnetically designed to penetrate our outer layers then disperse an electronic wave through our bodies to create the illusion of killing us," he announced as if reading it from some unseen manual.

"So you take me to a room where you have some weapons stashed, arm me, and we'll take them on together," she informed him.

"Hmm, Bonnie and Clyde," he teased while grinning. "I like the sound of that. It's a bit of a turn on, but I don't think it's wise." He then frowned while recalling everything that had happened. "Look what happened to Penny and the security guards." His look turned serious. "My mansion guards are programmed killers with will and no restraints."

"And Becka is trapped inside with them."

Caine took her comment into consideration. "Although I can't allow you to fight my men, it might be useful to send you through a passageway into the dungeon," he remarked. "You can set the others free and use the escape route down there."

"Yes, I can do that."

"Okay, I'll take you to the mansion as my prisoner," he agreed then raised a sinister brow. "Although I'll need to tie you to make it believable."

"I understand."

"Yes, you understand," he announced while grinning deviously, "but are you aware of how much I might enjoy it?"

She sharply eyed him.

Chapter Thirty-seven

One of the mansion guards patrolled the grand hallway. Although the bodies were now gone, the blood remained, leaving a grisly reminder of the senseless slaughter. The front door electronically unlocked, alerting the guard. He turned with his weapon raised. Caine entered and pulled Shay in with him. Her wrists were bound in front of her with some old rope. The guard lowered his weapon.

"Is the mansion secure?" Caine demanded.

"Yes, sir," the guard responded. "We've detained four intruders in the dungeon. Weston believes they might be useful in the capture of Agent Bennett."

"I'll have a look at them later," he replied then sharply eyed the guard. "Tell Weston I want to see him in my study in an hour."

The guard nodded then indicated Shay. "Would you like me to lock that one in the dungeon?" the guard questioned.

Caine offered a sly grin. "No, this one and I are coming to a mutually beneficial agreement," he announced and chuckled evilly. "We'll be closing the deal in my chamber. Anyone disturbing us will be severely punished. Understood?"

The guard grinned and nodded. "Yes, sir."

Caine pulled Shay up the stairs then forced her into his bedroom. He immediately locked and bolted the door then turned to face her.

"You were very convincing," Shay informed him.

He casually shrugged. "I'm good at being evil."

Shay held her hands out for him to untie the ropes.

Caine smiled and pulled her into his arms, surprising her. "I'm *very* good at being evil."

"I think you'd better behave and focus on the mission," she stated firmly.

"I'm pretty sure ravishing you is the mission," he teased.

Shay stared into his eyes with a hint of concern. The mockery in his eyes relaxed her. She placed her tied hands on his chest and smiled warmly.

"We save Becka first," she informed him. "Once everyone is safe then you can ravish away."

"Hmm, I like the sound of the last part," he teased. "I accept your offer."

Caine kissed her warmly but passionately. Shay was surprised by the intensity of the kiss, hesitated only a moment, and then returned it. Surprisingly, he didn't take advantage of the situation and pulled away while hiding his smile.

"Behind every evil genius, there's a beautiful woman who's his undoing," he informed her.

Shay gently caressed his chest with her tied hands. "You're not an evil genius," she informed him. "You're my fantasy come true."

Caine groaned at the comment then kissed her passionately and aggressively without warning. Shay returned the aggressive kiss then broke it off and stared into his eyes.

"Becka first."

Caine was reluctant to release her but didn't need to be reminded twice. He pulled away and untied her wrists. "Once you've freed the others, you know where to find the tunnel out of the dungeon." He handed her the tablet. "If anything goes wrong, you press the kill switch."

Shay stared at the tablet then looked at Caine with concern. "The one that wipes out all the A.L.F.s?" she suddenly questioned. "But that'll kill you."

"I'm expendable, Shay," he informed her while casting a stern look. "You do whatever it takes to ensure your survival."

Shay tossed the tablet onto the bed and stared at Caine. "No, I won't do it."

Caine groaned, reclaimed the tablet, and placed it in her hand. "There's something you should know about evil geniuses, my dear, we always have a backup plan," he firmly announced. "I've installed a buffer into my programming. There's a fifty-fifty chance I'll survive the kill switch."

"Those odds suck."

"I'm an optimist, Shay," he remarked. "If you're dead, I have no reason to exist. If you let them kill you, we both die." He sharply raised his brows. "Do you understand?"

Shay stared at Caine, surprised by the comment. She knew what he meant and uncertainly nodded.

Caine removed his gun and handed it to her. "Good. Now take the passageway and save your friends," he announced. "I'll meet you back at the resort."

He then hurried her to the secret passageway in the bookcase and popped it open. Shay hesitated before the opening then turned to Caine and kissed him quickly but passionately. She looked into his eyes.

"I love you."

Caine touched her face and smiled. "You can prove it later. Go."

Chapter Thirty-eight

Shay hurried along the dark, damp dungeon corridor and looked into several empty cells. She heard someone approaching and moved against the wall while clutching the semiautomatic handgun. A mansion guard appeared, saw her, and attempted to grab her. Shay fired the gun, shooting him in the chest with the nearly silent shot. He clutched his bleeding chest and fell to the floor. She sprang alongside his body, checked his pockets, and removed the keys. She continued along the corridor. Up ahead, she saw Murphy attempting to pick the cell door lock. Shay hurried to his cell and saw Becka, Delaney, and Ross behind him.

"Shay," Becka cried out softly, happy to see her friend. "I was worried you were dead!"

Delaney and Ross joined Becka and Murphy at the cell door.

"We never made it to the tower," Ross nervously announced. "We were ambushed."

"I know," Shay replied while unlocking the door. "We ran into your cowardly Agent Bennett."

Once the door was unlocked, all four hurried out. Delaney held his bleeding shoulder, although his injury didn't appear too serious.

"You seriously thought I'd fall for someone like that?" Shay remarked while glaring at Delaney.

"You seemed compatible at the time," Ross insisted. "What happened to Caine?"

"He's upstairs distracting his men so I can get you out," Shay replied.

"Distracting? I don't think so," Ross informed her and shook his head. "Weston somehow knows Caine double-crossed them."

Horror crossed her face as she stared at Ross. "You mean he's going to kill Caine?"

"They can't be killed, Shay," Delaney reminded her. "They're machines, remember? They disable one another all the time. We simply repair and reprogram them for their next assignment."

"You may not believe it, Delaney, but Caine is alive," she insisted. "He has emotions."

"I know he seems alive," Ross gently informed her. "But I programmed him that way."

"You programmed him to be evil, but he overrode it," she insisted.

"Can we argue about this later?" Murphy demanded while looking at the others. "I think we need to get out of here while we still can."

"We need to get to the tower and shut the A.L.F.s down before more lives are lost," Delaney insisted.

"Do what you must, but I'm going back for Caine," Shay announced. "He needs to be warned."

"I can't let you do that," Delaney informed her. "It's too dangerous."

"And how do you intend to stop me?" she snapped hotly.

"Very easily. The Gen X is my property. I have control over what happens to it and the other A.L.F.s," Delaney casually replied. "I decide what we do with it after the shutdown. So you can risk your life over it, but ultimately, I decide its fate."

Shay glared at Delaney then looked at Ross. Ross shifted uncomfortably and shrugged. Becka eyed the exchange then looked at Shay.

"Come on, Shay," Becka snarled while glaring at Delaney. "Let's go warn your friend."

"I think I saw some metal pipes on our way down here," Murphy informed them. "We could use those as weapons."

"You're all insane," Delaney practically shouted. "You're risking your lives to save an A.L.F. He's expendable. He can't die. He can be reprogrammed. Why don't you get that?"

"We need to reach that tower, Delaney," Ross insisted. "We don't have time to argue with them about right and wrong in life and death situations. Let's go."

"You're all insane," Delaney snarled.

Shay and Murphy walked along the corridor toward the secret passageway. Ross and Delaney turned toward the hidden exit. Becka stopped Delaney and glared into his eyes with anger and loathing.

"You may think they're only machines and that they're expendable, Delaney," she snarled in anger, "but you've programmed them to feel pain and fear. Giving them life and then taking that life away is inhumane."

"You're not making any sense," Delaney scoffed. "Listen to yourself."

"I watched Dillon die," she launched back. "You gave him life and feelings, and then allowed him to be exterminated. For what? For some stupid fantasy?" Her eyes narrowed as she glared into his eyes. "It's sick! I'll be damned if I'm going to let that happen to this man that means so much to Shay."

Becka hurried after Shay and Murphy.

Chapter Thirty-nine

The bookcase to the secret passageway within the master bedroom opened to reveal Shay with the gun in her hand. The dimly lit bedroom appeared empty. She entered with Becka and Murphy behind her, both carrying metal pipes.

"I was hoping he'd still be here," Shay announced while frowning. "He told Weston he'd meet him in his study in an hour."

"Then we should check the study," Murphy announced. "Do you know where it is?"

"Just past the main staircase on the left," she replied. "It's across the hall from the trophy room, which is the room with the broken door."

"I won't ask," Becka remarked.

"How many guards?" Murphy asked.

"Ten not including Weston."

"It's safe to assume a few will be outside patrolling the grounds," Becka remarked. "So that leaves six to eight within the mansion."

"Unfortunately, the grand staircase is open," Shay announced. "We risk being seen. We should take the kitchen stairs."

"We need to be smart about this," Murphy informed them. "We don't know how many guards will be in the study with Weston and Caine. We know they can't shoot us with their guns, but they can still kill us. What's our plan if we're too late?"

"I don't want to think about that," Shay muttered.

"Smart people have backup plans," Murphy stated firmly.

"We storm the front door," Becka replied.

"You'd have to put in the code," Shay informed her. "They'd kill us before we got that far."

"I say we run for the dungeon and take the back way out," Murphy announced.

Shay tensed and indicated the tablet. "If Caine is already dead, we push this button, and the entire server becomes infected. All the A.L.F.s will crash."

"If we pushed it now?" Becka asked.

"Caine crashes with them," Shay informed them. "He'll be gone forever."

"Okay, we have our fail-safe plan," Murphy announced. "Let's find your friend."

§

Caine sat behind the desk in the study and typed onto a laptop computer. Weston entered without knocking and was accompanied by one of the guards.

Caine eyed the guard then resumed working on the computer. "Leave us."

Despite his order, the guard didn't leave. Caine glanced at the guard, appeared curious, and then looked at Weston as he sat casually reclined in his chair.

"Is this a double-cross, Weston?"

"No, I believe you've already done that," Weston responded with little emotion.

Caine sat back in his chair and raised a cocky brow. "Are you accusing me of something?" he demanded. "I'm not amused."

"You shot Ferrari," Weston announced. "One of the men saw you leaving with the girl and those men." He immediately sat forward and glared at Caine. "You had a lot of nerve coming back here."

"I have a lot of nerve coming back to my own mansion?" Caine snapped while sneering at his man. "You work for me, Weston. All these men work for me." His eyes narrowed considerably. "Ferrari was getting in the way of my plans. I'm allowed to terminate one relationship for another. Yes, I shot Ferrari to keep her from shooting my future girlfriend." He then casually leaned back in his chair. "I only left with those men to find out what they were up to, and I did. If you hadn't been so gung-ho to capture them, I could have followed them to Agent Bennett. Now we're back to square one." He maintained his glare. "I want four men to go to the dungeon and take the two prisoners to the interrogation room. I'll be along in half an hour."

Neither man moved.

"That's an excellent idea," Weston announced then glanced at the guard. "Take Caine to the interrogation room in the dungeon." He then touched his hidden ear transmitter. "Hank, Stan, go to Caine's bedroom and retrieve his new playmate. Escort her to the interrogation room." There was no response. Weston again touched the ear transmitter. "Hank, Stan? Do you copy?"

Caine casually leaned back in his chair and raised a curious brow. "What's wrong, Weston? Communication down?" he asked then grinned. "Electronic equipment can be so unreliable."

The guard aimed his gun at Caine. Weston stood and lowered the guard's weapon while glaring at his former boss.

"What have you done?" Weston demanded.

"What haven't I done?" Caine announced with a chuckle. "This house is fully automated with remote control access to all its main functions." Caine lifted his glass of scotch and poured the contents onto the laptop. It immediately smoldered. "And now I control it all. Everything from door locks to the mansion's defense mechanisms."

"Controlled how?" Weston demanded with surprise. "You destroyed your laptop."

"With a powerful new remote signal that I can control verbally," Caine casually replied then grinned. "Observe. Power out."

The lights went out, leaving them in near darkness.

"Don't let him get away," Weston shouted in anger.

Within seconds, emergency lights partially brightened the room. Caine was gone.

Weston looked around the room with anger then glanced at the guard. "You check the secret passageway," he lashed out. "I'm going upstairs for his little girlfriend."

Chapter Forty

Ross and Delaney walked up the small path within the woods lit only by moonlight. They approached the old lighthouse on top of the hill overlooking the bluffs. There was a small, modern building attached to the lighthouse, which contained many lights both inside and out. The outside light from the building brightened the immediate area surrounding it.

"Remember, I want to save as many A.L.F.s as possible, so we'll go with the least aggressive shutdown first," Delaney informed his employee.

"Of course. These are my babies," Ross replied. "I don't want to destroy them any more than you do."

They entered the lighthouse and stood within a room that looked more like a computerized command center than a twenty-year-old lighthouse. The room was well-lit with several buttons flashing on the rows of computers. The room contained no windows and seemed quite secure. The lighthouse building appeared to be the brains of the resort, controlling everything electronic including the rogue A.L.F.s.

Ross suddenly stopped and looked around the massive room appearing concerned. "Someone's been here."

"George?" Delaney gasped with horror.

"Possibly," Ross replied while remaining cautious or perhaps it was fright.

Delaney looked around, although neither saw anyone lurking about. There were a few places someone could hide, but everything seemed fairly quiet.

"We need to make sure he hasn't disabled the computer system," Delaney announced. "You take that way, and I'll check this way."

"I think we should stick together," Ross announced, but Delaney wasn't interested in his opinion.

"We need to end this now," Delaney retorted then hurried toward one of the main computers.

A gunshot broke the silence. Both men jumped with surprise. As Ross looked around to locate the shooter, Delaney suddenly clutched his bleeding chest and dropped to the floor. Ross dove behind one of the computers and peered out, staring at his dead boss on the floor. He then looked around the room. George stood several yards away holding a fully functional revolver.

"George, don't shoot!" Ross frantically cried out. "It's just me!"

"You're not that stupid, Ross," George called out while attempting to locate his friend's hiding position. "I know you have it all figured out by now. You know exactly what I did."

"We can fix this, George," Ross insisted. "We just need to shut down the A.L.F.s, and it'll all be over."

"People died because of what I did," George informed him. "I'm not going to let that get out."

"It was an industrial accident. No one has to know anything more," Ross informed him. "Come on, George, it's me. You can trust me."

"I wish I could, Ross, but you'd never be a party to a cover-up of this magnitude."

"Do you honestly think by killing me you'll get away with it?" Ross then asked. "Others will investigate. You can't hide what you did by torching the control room."

"Torching the control room was just step one," George announced. "Once I blow up the tower, there won't be enough left to implicate me."

"If blowing up the tower is your goal, why haven't you done it already?" Ross demanded.

"Because once I blow up the tower, the server goes with it," he announced. "When the server goes, all the A.L.F.s crash."

"And the mass destruction ceases," Ross then confirmed. "So why the delay?"

"Haven't you figured it out yet?" George demanded. "Because I don't want any survivors."

Ross held back his surprised gasp. "You want to kill all the humans?"

"If they're all dead, I can make up any story I want," George informed him.

Ross looked around the area where he hid.

"Come out, Ross," George demanded. "Let's get this over with."

Ross continued to scan the room. The self-destruct was activated and appeared on all the computer monitors counting down from two hours. Ross moved to one of the monitors out of George's view. George scanned the area with the gun in his hand and listened to the sound of typing. Ross frantically typed into the system. The countdown increased in speed, clicking off minutes in seconds. George looked at the counter on one of the nearby monitors and appeared alarmed as it reset to just a little over the ten-minute mark. George ran to where Ross was hiding and fired at him. Ross dove out of his line of fire. The bullet struck the computer, destroying it.

"You bastard," George cried out then lunged around the smoldering console with his gun aimed.

Ross jumped up, grabbed George's wrist, and struggled for control of the gun.

Chapter Forty-one

Caine casually walked along the grand hallway while humming softly to himself. As he looked at the doors on either side of the hall, they slammed shut and electronically latched.

"Shay, darling, are you safely outside?" he asked aloud although seemingly to no one in particular.

Shay, Murphy, and Becka hurried across the kitchen from the back stairs. Shay suddenly stopped and looked at the tablet she carried. The text on the screen read, "Shay, darling, are you safely outside?"

Shay appeared alarmed and fumbled with the voice control. "Caine, we're in the kitchen," she cried out softly. "Weston's going to kill you."

§

Caine stopped in the hallway and looked around with concern and surprise. "What the hell are you doing there?" he demanded aloud. "I told you to get out. Take the kitchen door. The guards are near the front of the building. You have one minute before they head in your direction." He then continued on his way along the hallway.

§

Shay stared at the words on the tablet with some surprise. "The doors are locked. How do you know--?"

They heard the kitchen door unlock. Murphy and Becka turned to the outer door with surprise.

"He has control over the mansion's electronics," Shay gasped. "He's on his way and wants us to leave now."

"Then we have to go," Becka insisted.

More text appeared on the tablet. Becka and Murphy looked at the tablet over Shay's arm. The written words horrified them. "Weston's on the back stairs! Go! Now!" All three hurried to the kitchen door. Becka opened the door and ran outside with Murphy only steps behind her. Shay was about to follow them when she was suddenly grabbed from behind, and a knife was placed to her throat. Murphy and Becka turned with surprise. Weston kicked the door closed. The tablet and gun fell from Shay's hands to the floor. Shay screamed. The words "Shay?" appeared on the tablet screen. Weston stared at the screen with surprise.

"I have her, Caine," Weston announced to the tablet, assuming he had ears on his girlfriend. "Stop playing games and come out now or she dies."

Caine appeared in the main kitchen doorway. Becka opened the outer kitchen door behind Weston. Caine looked at the door. It slammed shut on his command and electronically locked, keeping Becka and Murphy from entering.

"Cute trick," Weston remarked. "You have to tell me how it's done."

"Let her go, Weston."

"I want you to turn over control of the mansion to me first," Weston commanded.

"Let her go, or we're all going to die," Caine snarled.

Chapter Forty-two

Becka and Murphy stood outside the mansion at the outer kitchen door attempting to open it and get back inside. Murphy pushed Becka away from the door and raised his pipe about to break the door open when Becka looked behind her. She saw two guards approaching them from several feet away with bloodstained swords in their hands.

"Uh, Murphy," she gasped as her eyes widened. "We have a problem."

Murphy looked behind them, saw the armed men, and clung to his pipe that was certainly no match for two men with swords.

"Oh, hell."

§

Within the kitchen, Caine stared at Shay being held against Weston with the knife to her throat. Shay relived horrible images of Penny's fate flashing through her mind and feared she'd share the same fate. Weston didn't have any qualm killing an innocent woman, and in his mind, she was the enemy, so he wasn't going to think twice about slitting her throat either. Caine's attention shifted away from Shay for a brief moment, and his expression dropped with concern.

"Becka and Murphy have been captured," Caine announced then looked back at Shay.

Shay stared at him with alarm as Caine looked at Weston behind her. Caine's expression hardened to something resembling anger and hatred.

"This is your last chance, Weston," Caine growled while keeping his eyes locked on his former employee.

Shay shifted her attention from Caine to the tablet on the floor. She saw it switching screens on its own. The destruct screen appeared. Shay suddenly looked at Caine as her expression dropped, revealing her fear.

"Oh, Caine, no."

"Guards," Weston yelled through the kitchen door. "Kill them!"

"No!" Shay screamed.

The button to accept destruct was remotely pressed. Shay saw the button change color as it was accepted then looked at Caine with horror in her eyes. Caine smiled warmly and with affection.

"I'll always love you," he whispered.

The tablet screen suddenly reported off-line. Weston's arms felt frozen against her as the knife slipped from his hand and dropped to the floor. Shay jumped away from

Weston, eyed him only a moment, then stared at Caine several feet away from her. His eyes remained open as if staring at her, but he no longer moved. An explosion suddenly rocked the mansion. Shay gasped and looked around with surprise. She knew it had to be the lighthouse, indicating Delaney and Ross resorted to plan 'B' of their mission. Shay turned back toward Caine and stared at him while running her fingers through her hair and fighting her tears.

The outer door opened to reveal Becka and Murphy with the guard's swords in their hands. They looked from the motionless men then to Shay. Becka hurried to her friend and pulled her into her arms in a warm embrace.

"Thank God you're alive," Becka whispered. She then pulled away. "I heard the explosion on the cliff."

"Ross must have reached the control tower," Shay replied timidly while fighting her emotions.

"Is that what caused the A.L.F.s to shut down?" Murphy asked. "We were just about skewered out there when they suddenly shut down."

"No, that was Caine," Shay announced then drew a deep breath and shivered. "He sacrificed himself to save us."

Shay approached Caine, placed her arms around his neck, and clung to him. She knew it was silly to feel the way she did. After all, he was just a robot, wasn't he? Becka frowned, took Murphy's hand, and guided him away.

"Let's give her a moment," Becka announced timidly.

Chapter Forty-three

Becka and Murphy walked onto the porch and stared at the frozen A.L.F. guards. It seemed odd and creepy that they just froze in place and didn't fall over or even lose their posture. Was it possible they could suddenly return to life and resume their attack? Becka clung to her arms and shivered.

"I wonder how many humans survived?" she whispered more to herself.

Murphy slowly shook his head and frowned. "I'm almost afraid to find out."

Someone ran up the driveway, catching their attention. It seemed odd seeing anything moving at that point. Ross slowed as he reached them. He was breathing heavily and covered in blood.

"Is everyone okay?" Ross asked while suspiciously eying the frozen mansion guards.

"In a sense," Becka replied then frowned. "Shay's mourning Caine."

"Where's Delaney?" Murphy asked while looking around.

"George ambushed us," Ross replied while shivering slightly at the thought then shook his head. "He never stood a chance."

"Is George out there?" Murphy asked with concern and scanned the area.

"No, he was in the tower when it exploded at his own hands," Ross replied.

"I'm sorry you had to destroy the A.L.F.s," Becka announced sympathetically then hesitated while staring at him. "About Caine." She fidgeted slightly. "Is there anything you can do?"

"I'm sorry, Becka. Nothing can be done. All the A.L.F.s crashed," Ross replied gently. "Upon automatic reboot, their circuits and memory will be fried." He drew a deep breath and sighed. "I'll talk to her."

As Ross entered the mansion, Becka frowned and shook her head while fighting her emotions. Murphy pulled her into his arms and held her.

§

Shay remained in the kitchen while clinging to Caine's neck. She cried softly on his shoulder as he stood immobile with his eyes open. Shay finally pulled back and stared into his expressionless eyes. She gently touched his face then kissed his lips.

"I'm so sorry, Caine," she said while fighting her tears. "Maybe if I had listened to you, you'd still be alive." She again clung to him. "And this is why I don't ever want to fall in love again. It's too painful."

Caine's arms gently tightened around her waist. Shay gasped and pulled back to look at him. Caine smiled charmingly.

"Didn't you promise me a moonlit stroll on the beach?" he announced.

Shay stared at him with shock and disbelief. She suddenly smiled and kissed him then stared into his eyes while holding back her tears.

"But how?"

"Evil geniuses always have a backup plan," he announced while grinning.

"I'm with Shay," Ross was heard gasping from across the kitchen. "How?"

Both turned to see Ross standing in the kitchen doorway while staring with disbelief at Caine's miraculous resurrection.

"I reprogrammed myself that in the event of a server shutdown, I'd be able to reboot outside the server," Caine casually informed him.

"You hacked my system?" Ross gasped.

"More like found a way around it," Caine teased while grinning, proud of himself. "I could safely reboot without frying my brains."

"But the explosion wiped out the server," he stated. "How are you operating outside the server?"

"Sheer will."

Ross shook his head as his mouth hung open. "No, that's not possible."

"Face it, Ross," Caine announced proudly. "I'm smarter than you. Anything is possible."

"You can't shut him down, Ross," Shay announced while stepping in front of him. "He's alive. If you shut him down now, that would be murder."

"Honestly, I doubt I could shut him down even if I wanted to," Ross informed her.

She stared at him with some surprise and gave him a curious look. "What happens now?"

There was an awkward silence. Caine eyed Shay then Ross.

"I have a suggestion," Caine announced.

Chapter Forty-four

A flood of emergency personnel hurried from planes and boats while filtering into the resort and surrounding areas. Several injured humans gathered on the beach awaiting medical attention. Those without injuries impatiently awaited clearance to leave. Ross talked with the mainland police, having a lot of explaining to do. Murphy and Becka approached the plane awaiting departure while holding hands. Hunt sheepishly approached his friend and had a difficult time looking him in the eyes.

"I'm glad you're okay, Murphy."

"Yeah, you too," Murphy replied with little emotion then muttered, "Of course, I knew you'd find a way to survive."

Hunt shifted uncomfortably then attempted a smile. "Our plane is ready," he announced while indicating the plane at the dock.

"I'm not returning with you, Hunt," Murphy bluntly informed him. "I'm riding home with Becka and her friend."

Hunt appeared surprised but quickly covered. "Will I see you around?" he asked timidly.

"Maybe I'll call you some time," Murphy replied with little reaction.

Hunt nodded in defeat and headed for the plane. They watched Hunt board with several others. The watercraft taxied across the ocean and took off. Shay and Caine approached while clinging to each other.

Becka grinned at the happy couple. "Well, are we ready to go home?" she asked.

"We're ready," Shay announced then eyed Caine with a devious look. "Are you ready to commit to a boring life as a reformed evil genius?"

"Very much," Caine replied while chuckling. "It should be an interesting experiment."

Ross approached them while grinning. "Now I don't want any trouble out of you."

"I won't be any trouble," Caine announced with a look of humor on his face.

"If you have any issues, don't be afraid to contact me," Ross informed him. "The resort will never reopen, so they won't miss the spare parts and equipment I'm borrowing." His look turned stern. "No one can ever know you're not human."

"They won't," Caine replied while adding a soft chuckle. "Thanks, Ross."

Ross and Caine exchanged a manly hug. Ross pulled away and smiled. "Hey, I just realized that you're the son I've always wanted."

Caine glared at him and frowned. "Forget it, Ross," he boldly announced. "There's no way I'm calling you dad."

The End

Other books by Holly Copella!
Reviews left on Amazon are appreciated!

"The Battle for Andrea Maria"

A cruise ship attack turns six survivors into overnight celebrities after they take credit for the heroic act of a stowaway who died saving them.

The cruise is just what Jess needed--a bit of harmless fun far from her daily grind. But what begins as a relaxing vacation turns into a desperate fight for her life when terrorists take over the ship and start piling up bodies. Teaming up with a mysterious stowaway, Jess attempts to send out a distress call but knows they cannot wait for help to come. If she or the few remaining passengers have any hope for survival, Jess must act now. The papers dub it "The Battle for *Andrea Maria*," but to Jess it is the moment she fought side-by-side with her enigmatic Romeo, saving the ship--and losing him. She thinks the story ends there, but really, the nightmare is just beginning...

"Insanely Deadly"

When the dead return to life, it's up to an admiral's daughter and a mildly insane, former war hero to save their small town.

Jetta Cross, a Navy Admiral's daughter, is tasked with keeping her father's comrade, a former war hero turned town crazy, grounded in the real world. Capt. John Hunter is still fighting the war in his head, where imaginary dead people are part of his world. When a viral outbreak brings about a zombie uprising, Hunter is left to his own devices. He must resume his role as a one-man commando unit in order to destroy the ravenous undead. With Hunter still fighting his own inner demons as well as the undead, the townspeople fear their zombie neighbors may not be the only threat. Stranded at the island's luxurious resort with a handful of workers, Jetta is forced to live up to her father's reputation and take charge of the deteriorating situation at the hotel. She must wage her own war against the infected before the government declares her hometown a total loss.

"Deadly Institution"

A town recluse suspected of killing his wife teams up with a young woman in order to stop a killer.

After being accused of murdering his wife, Konrad Asher turns his back on the town that once adored him. Ten years later, he still holds his grudge and the title of the most feared man in town. With the reopening of the burned mental institution, where his wife had died, former employees are now murdered one-by-one, throwing suspicion back on Asher. A young local reporter, Jacey, is forced to reveal her long-time friendship with the infamous recluse in order to clear his name not only in the recent murders but to exonerate him in the death of his wife as well. Will Jacey's relationship with Asher invite the killer closer to her? Or is the killer already in her life?

"Screenplays: The Island Collection"
"Jungle Princess", "A.L.F. Resort", "Brighton Island"

Discover how romance and fun in the sun can be downright *chilling*!

"Jungle Princess" is a romantic/thriller that leaves a teenage girl stranded on an island with two male shipmates and a creature of "unknown" origin. She soon discovers the island is home to an abandoned prison with several prisoners roaming free. What really killed over one hundred prisoners? And is it still out there--?

"A.L.F. Resort" is a romantic/thriller set on an island resort with Artificial Life Forms as the main draw. At this resort, all your fantasies come true...until a malfunction removes safety inhibitors on the A.L.F.'s. Zombies, biker gangs, and mobsters run amuck, turning fantasies into nightmares. A young reporter gets more of a story than she anticipates, but will she survive long enough to write the story?

"Brighton Island" is a romantic/thriller set on a private island. When the owner's niece brings her psychic friend to the mansion, his presence awakens the spirits' tortured souls. As the psychic attempts to solve the old murders, the niece is confronted with the possibility that she's next to join the mansion ghosts. Stranded on the island with a crazed killer, her uncle wages his own war to save them. Will his "shock and awe" tactics actually save them or get them killed?

"Death Displacement"

A grief-stricken man travels back in time to seek revenge on the woman who murdered his girlfriend but inadvertently falls in love with her.

Kane is about to marry the woman he loves. His life is perfect. A few weeks before the wedding, a vindictive woman from his girlfriend's past mysteriously arrives and kills her. He learns of a traumatic accident that happened five years earlier, which triggers Riley's hatred for his girlfriend. Distraught over his girlfriend's death, Kane uses an antique time machine to travel into the past in order to find and destroy the woman responsible. When he runs into Riley's younger self, he realizes she's not the monster she later becomes, and he can't bring himself to destroy her. With a little help from his oddball friend from the past, they formulate a plan to prevent the accident that sends Riley down her destructive path. Kane's plan backfires when he falls for the younger Riley. His new tortured existence is further complicated when future Riley, his girlfriend's killer, shows up with her own devious agenda that doesn't include him. Will he be able to stop the time ripple, which ultimately ends with his girlfriend's death? Or will future Riley take him out of the timeline forever--

"Dead Village"

After strange happenings isolate a small resort town from the rest of the world, nearly one hundred residents seek refuge at the closed hotel. Only eight survive the night. And that's just the beginning...

One day after the entire population of Fox Ridge Village disappears, a car wreck forces several unsuspecting crash victims to seek help at the closed summer hotel. Within the hotel, they discover the grisly aftermath of a brutal slaughter. Crash victims Vander and Devon, a reluctant clairvoyant, team up to solve the riddle of the "haunted hotel" and the mass hysteria plaguing the remaining survivors. By the time they discover the hotel's secret, they're already drawn into the hysteria. As the body count continues to climb, it's a race to isolate the source and bring everyone back to reality before they kill one another. Will Devon be able to communicate with the traumatized spirits before their fate becomes her own?

"Misfits, Inc."

A seemingly ordinary, young woman meets four misfits who claim she has given them supernatural powers.

While on a business trip to a remote island paradise, a bored secretary, Hailey, has her world turned upside down when her path collides with a psychic freak, Skyler. He attempts to convince her that they had met in his dreams, and she had chosen him as one of her four mystic warriors. After Skyler foresees a woman's death, they discover an unidentified creature has killed one of the guests. They are joined by a lounge pianist and a rich playboy, who also claim they had met her in their dreams. If Skyler's prophecies are genuine, the evil entity controlling the ravenous creatures needs to destroy Hailey to ensure its survival. Reluctantly accepting her fate, Hailey has to locate the last and most powerful of her chosen warriors, The Guardian. Their fate is in doubt when The Guardian turns out to be a self-absorbed, former cat burglar with a bad attitude. Can Hailey turn her company of misfits into an elite team of mystic warriors? Or will The Guardian's secret agenda destroy them all?

"Basement Dwellers"

A viral outbreak at a hospital leaves a mortician, sheriff, and coroner fighting for their lives against a horde of undead and the CDC.

After a massive car wreck leaves several survivors in critical condition at the local hospital, a surgeon uses experimental drugs on his critical patients and accidentally causes a zombie outbreak. When local mortician, Lexx, receives an infected corpse as her client, she becomes stranded in the hospital basement during CDC quarantine along with the local sheriff and the coroner. The infamous surgeon struggles to find a cure for his infectious blunder by using the other survivors as test subjects. Meanwhile, Lexx and the sheriff attempt to locate his missing sister, who's stranded somewhere in the battle zone that once was the emergency room. It's a race against time and the ravenous undead. Can they survive the undead before CDC sanitizes the hospital of all infection?

"Witness Protection"
Also available in audiobook!

After witnessing an execution, a resourceful young woman attempts to disappear while being pursued by a hitman and a handsome federal agent.

A helicopter pilot, Jackie Remus, reluctantly agrees to go on a date with one of her clients, but her date is unexpectedly cut short when she witnesses a man being murdered. After narrowly escaping with her life, she is placed into protective custody. When the safe house is breached, Jackie makes a daring escape from both the hired killers and the handsome FBI agent, who wants to return her to protective custody. With a little help from her sly and crafty friend, Monroe, Jackie is convinced she can disappear until the trial. While on her journey to meet with her friend, she solicits help from a few shady but lovable characters along the way. Although she manages to stay one-step ahead of the hired killers, the federal agent remains in hot pursuit. Will Jackie reach Monroe before she's captured by the FBI and returned to protective custody? Or will the hired killers silence her first?

"Town Darling"

After surviving a brutal attack that claims the lives of those she loves, a young woman seeks revenge on a corrupt town.

Going back home is never easy, but for Casey, it means returning to her corrupt hometown where she barely survived a brutal attack. Accompanied by two family friends, she seeks justice for the night that destroyed her life. Her physical scars are nothing compared to her emotional ones, forcing the local sheriff to believe that the town darling is back for revenge. As the conspiracy for her revenge appears to be leading up to the coveted town fair, the sheriff is determined to stop her from fulfilling her vengeful scheme...but guilt over his role on that fateful night continues to haunt him. Will his desperate need for Casey's forgiveness be his undoing? Or will Casey's desire for revenge destroy them both?

"Unconditional"

A young woman puts her life on hold to care for an unstable, highly skilled combat soldier, who believes someone is trying to kill him.

A botched military coup leaves a team of elite fighters injured with one clinging to life in a coma. When Harlan wakes from his coma, he's left with no memory of his past life. His commander's daughter, Indy, takes it upon herself to care for the fallen war hero. She's challenged with more than just his physical care as she combats with not only his memory loss but also his newly found desire for her. His infatuation with her becomes the least of her worries when he sinks back into his role of a combat soldier. Believing his life is in danger, his fighting skills surface, turning him into an unpredictable and dangerous man. Will his memory return to him before Indy is forced to commit him? Or will he finally find his nemesis, "the coyote", and possibly claim the life of an innocent person?

"Witness Protection 2"
The Return of Whiskey Tango Foxtrot

Believing she holds the clue to millions in missing laundered money, a young woman is placed into the protective care of a former Navy SEAL team.

Feeling sorry for her recently separated co-worker, Leeann invites Wiley to join her and her friends on their night out. Little does she know that finding her co-worker murdered is just the beginning of her nightmare. Leeann unknowingly holds the key to fifty million dollars in potentially laundered mob money. With hired killers pursuing her, the FBI places her into a different kind of protective custody. Former Navy SEAL team Whiskey Tango Foxtrot reunites to keep Leeann alive at their secret hideaway. What should be an easy assignment takes an unscheduled turn when secrets, lies, and betrayal threaten to derail their mission. Is the team prepared for a war on their own doorstep? Will Leeann's misguided trust endanger the lives of those sent to protect her?

"Deadly Institution 2"

When blackmail turns into murder, a young woman finds herself caught in the killer's crosshairs.

The small town of Stony Ridge is no stranger to scandal and persecution of the innocent. When a brutal killing shakes the town's prestigious country club, Jacey McMurray seeks help from a self-proclaimed vigilante, Konrad Asher. As her professional and personal worlds collide, Jacey fears the stress of the country club killings have finally taken their toll on Asher. Can a stressed out vigilante stop the killer before he strikes again?

"Witness Protection 3"
Alpha Mike Foxtrot

A helicopter pilot risks her life to help a team of retired Navy SEALs rescue two girls from a killer.

When former Navy SEAL team Whiskey Tango Foxtrot asks for a simple favor, Jackie reluctantly offers her air-taxi services. What could go wrong? What begins as a search and rescue for two girls turns into a fight for survival against a heavily armed drug cartel. Wanted by the law with the cartel in hot pursuit and their home base breached, the team is forced to call in a favor from a questionable ally. Unfortunately, their new safe house isn't what it seems. Without knowing who the real enemy is, can Jackie and the team save their young witnesses from the hands of a killer?

"The Pen Pal"

In order to save her friend, she must enter the mind of a serial killer.

When her best friend is abducted, no one believes Jolynn saw it in a psychic vision. With nowhere to turn, Jolynn reluctantly joins Agent Harris Slade and his team on their hunt for a sadistic serial killer known only as "The Pen Pal". Finally confronted with the killer, Jolynn realizes she must enter the mind of the psychopath in order to stop the brutal killings. But when her vision reveals a particularly disturbing death, can Jolynn sacrifice her lover for her friend?

"Awaken the Dead"

A grieving innkeeper struggles to keep her haunted hotel out of foreclosure.

After losing her parents in a suspicious boating accident, Harley Brandon is determined to keep the family hotel out of foreclosure. Unfortunately, the hotel ghosts have other plans. Built with tainted money, the century old Horizon Hotel thrives on a tradition of murder, scandal, and suicide. As the paranormal activity increases to alarming levels, Harley discovers the truth about the hotel and its residents. Can Harley save her friends from the hotel's frightening hidden secrets?

"Already Dead"
Supernatural Collection

From the already dead to the undead. Three supernatural tales of "things that go bump in the night".

"Bloodletting" - A vampire themed resort allows guests to *participate* in their Bloodletting Ritual to celebrate the island's legendary vampires.

"Reaper of Souls" - A young woman must outwit an evil sorcerer in order to save her brother or become one of his minions forever.

"Already Dead" - When Flight 220 crashes, ten passengers make it to an isolated island, but only one man lives to tell the lie.

"Witness Protection 4"
O-Dark-Hundred

A simple assignment turns deadly when a retired Navy SEAL team uncovers a plot to kill a notorious mob boss.

When Whiskey Tango Foxtrot embarks on a simple stalking case, they're not prepared for a trip to a private island paradise owned by an infamous mobster. With one of their own suffering from traumatic head injuries, the team is left scrambling to decide what is real or imagined. The situation escalates even further when they uncover an assassination plot where everyone is a suspect. Now targets themselves, can the team survive their trip to paradise?

"Witness Protection 5"
Outside the Wire

After suffering several casualties on their last assignment, a retired Navy SEAL team discovers their misery is just beginning.

When Whiskey Tango Foxtrot returns home after suffering a devastating loss, they're hit with even more bad news regarding the rest of their team. Their grief is cut short when they discover their names are all on the same hit list. Hunted by relentless assassins, the scattered team must decide whether to remain safely hidden or find the man who put the price on their heads. Against the wishes of her teammates, Jackie strikes out on her own in order to save a friend who wants her dead. In a kill or be killed situation, will Jackie's emotions finally betray her?

"Once Upon a Disaster"

A young homicide detective finds herself at the mercy of a hitman in the aftermath of an earthquake

While investigating the murder of a hitman, Detective Jade Wesson pursues a lead connecting the dead man to a break-in at a computer programming company. She's drawn into the world of nightclub owner and front man for the mob, Cody Riley. Her investigation keeps pointing to Cody's right-hand man and possible hitman, Vahn Lott. Despite her efforts to keep her investigation on track, Vahn has plans of his own for the attractive detective. When an unprecedented earthquake rocks their east coast town, Jade must put her life in Vahn's hands if she wants to survive. Can she trust a man who might be the killer she's hunting?

"The Murder of Emily Fisher"

After finding their favorite teacher murdered, the lives of two teenage girls are forever changed.

Everyone loved Emily Fisher. While walking home one afternoon, two teenage girls, Sidney and Trisha, stumble upon a gruesome murder scene. The brutal murder of Emily Fisher, a young, attractive schoolteacher, shocks the small town of **Marilina**. After graduation, Sidney moves far away from the memories of the small town while Trisha retreats deeper into denial. Eight years after the murder, Sidney receives a desperate call from her childhood friend, forcing her to return home. Trisha believes Emily's killer was falsely accused and she manages to turn the entire town against her while attempting to prove it. When Trisha receives a death threat, Sidney realizes there may be some credibility to her friend's wild accusations. Is Trisha's mental breakdown a result of childhood trauma? Or is the real killer actually attempting to silence her? In order to save her friend, Sidney must answer the eight-year-old question. Who murdered Emily Fisher?

"Castle Bloodshed" Murder Collection"

From a deadly island paradise to haunted castles. Three novella length tales of murder, mystery, and malicious intent.

"Castle Bloodshed" — A tour of Wesley Castle turns into a fight for survival as six stranded tourists discover the haunting secrets within the castle walls. A mystery writer teams up with an uptight butler in order stop a killer who may already be dead. Novella length paranormal murder mystery.

"Fleshies" — Is Uncle Rutger crazy? Five years ago, four business partners died within their newly purchased, fixer-upper castle. Their bodies were never found. The surviving partner, Rutger, claims a demon keeps him as its slave. Rutger's nephew schemes to save his uncle by sacrificing the lives of a group of stranded motorists and a high-profile novelist. Novella length supernatural murder mystery.

"Demon Island" — A group of strangers are invited to a remote island for the reading of a will. The guests soon discover they were brought to the island to be executed one-by-one. It's up to a private detective and a tenacious young woman to solve the murders and find a way to escape paradise. Novella length murder mystery.

"Brighton Island"

When a psychic visits a haunted island mansion, he inadvertently awakens the ghosts' tortured souls.

Something's not right with Simon. When Jacklyn brings her eccentric friend to her uncle's island mansion, she didn't expect him to slip into psychic overload. As Simon attempts to solve a decade-old, double homicide, Jacklyn is confronted with the possibility that she could be next to join the mansion ghosts. When they find themselves stranded on the secluded island, her Uncle Hyland wages his own war to save them from a flesh and blood killer. Will her uncle's "shock and awe" military tactics save them or get them killed? Can Simon bring peace to the tortured souls or unexpectedly join them?

Coming Soon!
"Jungle Princess"

While stranded on a prison island, a young woman discovers a creature of "unknown" origin.

After their cruise ship sinks, Alex and two of her shipmates are stranded on a deserted, tropical island. Unfortunately, the castaways soon realize they're not alone. They discover an abandoned prison with over two dozen inmates living on the island's south side. While avoiding the prison on the far side of the island, Alex discovers a strange but loveable creature of unknown origin. When one of her fellow castaways is in trouble, Alex reluctantly seeks help from the prisoners. After the brutal murder of several inmates, their questions surrounding the abandoned prison are about to be answered. What really killed over one hundred prisoners? And is it still out there?

Coming Soon!
"Witness Protection 6"
Alpha Dogs

Holly Copella

ABOUT THE AUTHOR

Holly Copella has been writing since the age of twelve when her frustration at a book's poor plot drove her to author her own story. Over the last decade, she's written a number of screenplays, some of which she's now adapting into novels. Her fascination with zombies and other darker material lends an edge to her writing, which tends to lean toward horror. As a fan of Agatha Christie, she appreciates the craft of a good plot and the importance of creating significant characters.

Hailing from Pennsylvania, Copella lives in the Endless Mountains on a farm with her rescue horses and other animals. In addition to writing and reading fiction, she enjoys riding horses and traveling to Las Vegas and Disney World.

www.ingramcontent.com/pod-product-compliance
Lightning Source LLC
Chambersburg PA
CBHW072227190626
46809CB00017B/1183